I0671348

INTO THE BRAMBLES

DANIEL ROY GREENFELD

Copyright © 2015 Daniel Roy Greenfeld, Audrey Roy Greenfeld, and Two Scoops Press.
All Rights Reserved

Published April 9, 2015 by Two Scoops Press
Paperback Edition
Book 1
Version 1.1

Edited by Audrey Roy Greenfeld
Cover art by Audrey Roy Greenfeld

This is a work of fiction. Names, characters, places, and incidents either are the product of the author's imagination or are used fictitiously, and any resemblance to actual persons, living or dead, events, or locales is entirely coincidental.

Except for the use of brief quotations in a review, no part of this publication may be reproduced, stored in retrieval system, copied in any form or by any means, electronic, mechanical, photocopying, recording or otherwise transmitted without written permission from the publisher.

Read more about this book and Daniel's other fiction writing efforts at danielroygreenfeld.com.

To the wife of my life,
Audrey Roy Greenfeld

TABLE OF CONTENTS

INTRODUCTION

The world was ancient, littered with the remains of a thousand wars. Over the aeons, gods, immortals, and heroes waged constant conflict against each other for thousands of years. The world was ravaged and sundered. Civilizations fell. Reptilians, utari, and mabden went extinct, only to be replaced by new species such as saurians and wolves. Old grudges never faded. The suffering was endless.

The Twenty-Second Age closed with the destruction of yet another Dark Lord in a long line of power-hungry beings intent on dominating the world. A new age dawned, the Twenty-Third Age. This was prophesied to be an enlightened time that promised an endless era of peace and prosperity.

Less than a thousand years later, the Twenty-Third Age ended in bloody conflict.

CHAPTER 1

PEONY

Scratched by thistle and thorn, Peony pushed desperately through the bramble. It was getting late. The forest shadows were deepening, and the wind was picking up. If she and the other villagers didn't find Wren quickly, they would have to turn back. No comforting, illuminating fire was allowed in the forests; their overlords didn't allow it. They had perhaps half an hour left before they had to turn back. Peony's heart ached at the thought of her little toddler alone in the cold night.

Even though the sun hadn't set yet, already she could see the twin-tailed comet fill the sky. Arriving at the start of the year, it had come with disturbingly bad luck. The cows produced spoiled milk, a chicken laid a cockatrice the local knight-magistrate had to kill, goats produced two-headed kids, wolves and worse plagued the forests, and all too many stillborn babies had been born for anyone's comfort. If not for the blessings cast

DANIEL ROY GREENFELD

by the dryads, the just-planted crops would certainly fail. And now her youngest son was lost in the woods.

Other villagers searched with her, including her husband. They had spread out, but not so far that they couldn't hear each other. Some of them grumbled at her allowing the toddler to escape beyond the fields, but most of them understood. Peony had four other children. Sometimes children wandered off. This was especially true during harvest, when everyone in the village would come out to reap, collect, and store while the crops were fresh.

Finally breaking free of thistle and thorn, Peony shivered at an unexpected chill. Her foot sank into the ground. It was soft and spongy. She was at the edge of a marshy area. She looked down in disgust at the filth that would certainly be coating her shoe.

Next to her foot was a footprint. It was much smaller than hers, a toddler's footprint. It was followed by another tiny footprint across the soft, sucking ground. Lighter than her, little Wren had easily walked across the spongy surface. The soft area cut a clear path through the trees and thicket that made up the deep forest.

Peony called out to the others. "I found his trail!" she said.

There was no response. In fact, she couldn't hear anyone else anymore: not her husband, nor any of the other villagers.

She listened carefully, praying that no wolves lurked nearby. For a moment she was indecisive, hesitating to move forward on her own. But then she decided to pursue little Wren, knowing that she could lose him to the beasts of the marshland if she didn't find him tonight. If she found him, she could bring them both out of the forest. She followed his trail, gritting her teeth as she pulled her feet out of the muck with each step.

Her heart quailed at the thought of her son alone in the woods. Then, as the ground hardened, she heard his faint crying over the growing howl of the wind. He wasn't far away. She followed the sound of his cries into a large clearing, the edges marked by leafless trees and withered thicket.

Wren was sitting in the middle, illuminated by an early moon. Here he was, her little Wren. He had been born tiny and weak. His older siblings had been happy, healthy babies, but Wren had always been in need of extra care. Even his little sister, still a swaddled baby, had done better. Wren had always been the small one with faint cries. He often had refused to eat. Peony had doted over him, trying to make him healthy, to keep him alive. She loved her little Wren. Now, his little face was red from crying over the cold, hunger, and fear.

Peony sobbed and ran forward.

Her foot came down with an oddly familiar crunch. She froze and looked around.

The clearing was covered in bones. There were a few where she stood, and enough to make a carpet where Wren sat.

Something about this place was terribly wrong.

Seeing the bones around her, the grime that covered Wren's toddler-sized tunic and trousers had new meaning. It made Peony flinch at the thought of picking him up. She hesitated.

As she looked at Wren sitting on the pile of bones, he noticed that she was there. He cried louder. His arms reached towards her, begging for his mother to pick him up. Peony knew that she needed to get herself and Wren away. Her heart melting for him, she crossed the bones without further hesitation, scooping him into her arms. He clung to her with fierce devotion, screaming his fear into the wind.

"Don't worry, Mommy's here," Peony said, hugging him. Clutching her wailing child, she ran back the way she came, away from the bones and back across the spongy land. Retreading her steps, she took the marshy trail, praying that she could find her way back again. By the time she was through, the sucking grasp of the earth left her gasping.

All that remained for her now was to get through the endless maze of thorn and thistle.

Crossing it with both hands free had been a slow, sometimes painful effort. Now, holding Wren, Peony didn't know what to do. Shivering, she wished she had worn her winter coat instead of just a dress. She called out for her husband, her neighbors, anyone.

For a moment, only the rustle of leaves in the evening autumn wind answered her. Then she heard the distant, mournful howl of a wolf. Dread filled her heart.

Staying here would be certain death, now that her pleas for help had revealed her location to the wolves. Even if she kept silent, keeping a tired, hungry Wren quiet was impossible. Yet the alternative, getting through the thicket, would be difficult and painful.

Another howl pierced the deepening gloom.

She knew what she had to do, and waiting longer would make it harder.

With Wren in one arm, it took her a long minute to stuff her long, long braid of hair into the back of her dress. Looking up at her with his tear-streaked face, Wren wailed the whole time, piercing the fog and his mother's ears with the volume of his cries.

A wolf heard his cries and howled back.

She picked Wren up, clutching him tightly. Biting her lip, she backed into the thicket, keeping Wren safe. The sharp thorns stuck and tore cloth and skin, but she pushed on with the tenacity of a mother. Minutes later, scratched and bleeding, she emerged from this first painful barrier.

Tears flowed freely down her cheeks, but she didn't pause. Wren needed her to be strong. Turning forward, Peony rushed through the woods, slowing only to back through another bramble, and then another.

CHAPTER 2

DRAGON BONES

"Bull, wake up! Bull! Where are Ram and Wren?" Peony demanded.

Bull snapped awake from his doze under his favorite tree and looked up at Peony, his wife. She held their youngest daughter Protea, while their oldest daughter Dandelion carried a basket of food.

It was one of those summer days where after early morning it was too hot to work. As it was past planting and not yet harvest, the work was pretty light. In fact, today was the rest day for the week. For their day off, Bull had taken the boys to the pond outside the village. There, he sat under his favorite tree with a fishing rod and napped. As a teenager he had discovered the perfect sitting spot, a place near the water where he could situate himself on his back just right, in the roots of his tree. As he grew older and larger, the roots had grown with him. Now, the bulging muscles he had built with hard labor matched the thick roots of the tree. The tree was an old friend to him, one who didn't ever annoy or bother him.

A gentle breeze kept the heat of the day at just the right temperature. Bull happily languished the day away at the same pace as the gentle stream at his feet.

But there was one problem. Ram and Wren were nowhere to be seen.

Ram was six and Wren was five, which meant they shouldn't have gotten very far. Yet since Wren had gone missing in the woods a few years back, Peony had become desperate any time she thought that the little runt could be missing. Considering the scars she had earned while pulling Wren out of the woods, Bull couldn't blame her. This was why they had carefully explained to Ram that it was his duty to protect his slightly younger, much smaller brother.

Bull got to his feet and stretched his muscular arms to the sky. Normally he would have relished the stretch, but Peony was doing her best to glare at him. He looked into her pretty eyes. "Don't worry, they can't have gotten far," he said.

"I'm going to look downstream. I'm going to find them," Bull said. Then he said more gently to his wife as he pointed upstream, "Peony, why don't you take the girls in that direction?"

Peony spent another moment glaring at him. Then she took her daughters each by the hand, heading quickly up the river.

Satisfied with his decisiveness, Bull headed down stream. He quickly reached the place where a dense thicket of brambles blocked his way, forcing him to go into the forest. This took him away from the stream, in the direction he hoped his sons had taken. He called out their names as his long strides carried him forward.

After a couple of minutes, he could no longer stride forward comfortably, blocked by the man-height bramble that was the edge of the forest. He found the easiest way through and pushed in. That's where he saw their boys, just past the thicket.

Ram, older and large for his age, was lying motionlessly on the ground. Wren, younger and small for his age, sat cross-legged next to Ram, playing with something in the dirt.

Relieved but angry, Bull snapped at the children. "Wren! Ram! Why did you wander off?" he said.

Wren, completely absorbed by his play, jerked in surprise. He smiled up at his father. Ram didn't move, not even flinching at Bull's stern tone.

"Look Daddy!" Wren said happily. "We found dragon bones!"

Bull looked at what Wren held in his hands and felt his skin crawl. About the size of a chicken, the headless skeleton was held together by fragments of skin, ligament, feather, and worst of all, the scaly skin of a snake.

It was the corpse of the cockatrice that the knight-magistrate had killed just two years earlier.

The creature, a monster born from a prize-winning hen of all things, had been aggressive and poisonous. Upon hatching, it had killed its own mother. Feeding on the corpses of every chicken in the hen house, it had grown quickly. It had escaped the chicken coop when its unfortunate owner opened the little door one morning. The woman had died in moments, her last act being to scream in terror. Hearing her chilling scream, her husband and children had rushed outside, only to be killed by the same murderer of their wife and mother.

Across the village, livestock had bolted in panic. After discovering that the cockatrice could kill with a single touch, the villagers hid in their homes. For days they had kept windows and chimney flues closed, terrified of the monster that prowled the streets.

Finally, the knight-magistrate had come in full armor, chasing the cockatrice into the woods. He had killed the monster, leaving its corpse there for the crows. He had also shed his armor on the spot, leaving it to rust.

Ram wasn't sleeping. He appeared to be poisoned, probably dead. Wren, who should have been lying dead next to his brother, was instead playing with something that was dangerously evil even in death.

"Wren, put down the bones," Bull said quietly. The fear in his gut made him want to scream the command, but he didn't. Perhaps Wren hadn't touched the poisonous parts yet, and Bull didn't want to put the boy at further risk.

"Okay, Daddy," Wren said, dropping the skeleton that he was holding. Wren stood up. Then he gestured at his brother. "Ram is sleeping," he said.

Bull took Wren by the arm and pulled him away from the corpse of the cockatrice. He put him next to a tree and commanded the boy to stay there. Trembling, he knelt by the prostate Ram.

Bull checked him for signs of life. Ram's breathing was tiny, shallow, almost gone.

Bull picked up Ram, carefully juggling him to where he could hold him with one massive arm. He motioned to Wren, and the smaller boy came over to be picked up as well. Compared to the work that Bull did every day, the boys weighed almost nothing, but they were his sons and his life.

With his height and long legs, Bull stepped carefully out of the bramble. Once clear, he put Wren down. Then

DANIEL ROY GREENFELD

he picked up his pace and called out Peony's name. Without waiting for her reply, he headed to the village gate, his destination the healer. He didn't pause to explain when his family called back at him. Instead, he ran as fast he could to the healer. There was a chance, however slim, that Ram might live that day.

The healer wasn't home, so Bull ran down the street, still carrying little Ram. He found her where he expected, at the tavern. She sat in the shade of an awning, leaning back slovenly, mug in hand. Unlike most women, healers were always without children, usually unmarried. It was said that healing was a purchase that they made from the gods, fertility the price that they paid.

At another time, Bull would have relished sitting in the shade with her, smacking his lips after each draw on an ale-laden mug. Today he was desperate, heart breaking with every passing moment. His eyes were watering with tears that he couldn't let fall. If that dam broke, he wouldn't be able to stop weeping.

"He touched cockatrice bones," Bull said. "But he's still breathing, just barely."

The healer stood up with a jerk, knocking over her chair. "Let's go back to my house," she said, concern twisting her face. "We don't have much time. Follow me." She ran out of the tavern and down the road to her house, Bull following her.

"Will he live?" Bull asked.

She didn't answer, just throwing open her door in a rush. "Bring him in!" she called over her shoulder.

The healer's house was much smaller than the building Bull called home. It had a hearth, shelves bolted to the walls, two stools, a cot for sleeping, and a long table for working her craft on those too weak to stand or sit. At her gesture, Bull placed his dying son on the table.

"Will he live?" Bull asked again.

"I don't know," she admitted. She felt the boy's forehead. This close to her, Bull could smell the ale on her. He couldn't stand the smell, knowing her penchant for drinking might mean his son's demise. "I thought that touching a cockatrice meant death. I'll do what I can, and with the grace of the gods he might live. Maybe."

"To which god should we pray?" Bull asked.

"To which god shouldn't you pray?" she retorted. She began pulling jars of unguents from the shelves that lined her home. "Give me space. Keep everyone out. No distractions. When it gets to suppertime, bring me bread and cheese. I need to be able to eat easily."

Bull nodded. He backed out of her home. He then turned to face his wife as she arrived with their other children in hand.

"She's doing what she can," he told Peony as he sank to his knees. "In the meantime, all we can do is pray."

CHAPTER 3

THE PYRE

Ram lived.

His parents were grateful that Ram lived, but Ram's recovery had not gone well. The boisterous boy was gone. In his place was a quiet child who looked up to his little brother.

Outside the healer's home, again and again Peony berated him for his failure until Bull could not take it anymore. Being a gentle soul, he didn't raise a hand to her. Instead, for the first time ever, Bull raised his voice. He screamed at her, his rage and guilt pouring out. But watching her cower with fear just made him feel worse. Disgusted with himself at many levels, Bull fled his family.

As he ran away, he heard Peony's sobbing. He also heard the children's cries of dismay. He was the cause of all this, his wastrel ways. Despair and self-loathing filled his heart. He wished he had a way to fix his mistakes, or at least a way to do penance for his failure as a father.

In the name of penance, Bull ran to his shed to get his wheelbarrow, in which he placed his woodcutting axe and shovel. Then he rushed to the temple, let go of the wheelbarrow, and smashed open the door with his brawny shoulder.

Inside, he went into the temple storage closet, lifted a heavy pottery jar of expensive holy oil, and carried it laboriously to the wheelbarrow. This done, he walked back into the temple and to the altar. He took the small, ornate eternal lamp from its resting place on the altar. Enchanted by a dryad priest long before he was born, the lamp was used to light the hearth fires of the village. He had never touched the lamp before; it was made of brass, yet wondrously light and warm as a pleasant bath. This too he placed in the wheelbarrow next to the axe, shovel and temple oil.

Robbery of the temple was a terrible crime, but with the despair of a father, he didn't care.

He left the village, passing through the gate in the wall. His haste perked the interest of the village dogs and they followed him. From the gate he went to his favorite tree. The tree, his old friend since childhood, had betrayed him. Now it had to die. He knew that the dryads could take his life for chopping it down, but he didn't care. Even without taking breaks, he worked for many hours, going deep into the night to finish his self-appointed task. He brought the tree down, chopping it up into pieces small enough for him to lift. His hands blistered on the wooden axe handle, yet he did not pause in his labor. He only slowed to sharpen the blade when he felt it dull.

Some of the villagers had come to watch him. No one had intervened. He heard them mutter about his taking of temple goods without the permission of the mendicant priest who visited every other week. His family wasn't present. For that he was grateful. He couldn't face Peony. As the hours passed, everyone returned to inside the village walls. Even the village dogs wandered off.

An hour after dusk, Bull heard the closing of the village gate. This was later than usual, but tonight was unusual. He continued in his labors.

Long into the night he chopped and broke up the wood. He would take breaks from chopping, lifting the pieces and stacking them to be burned in one great bonfire. Finally, twelve hours after Bull had screamed at his wife, he was done. He had his pyre.

He dropped the axe and picked up the shovel in one blistered hand. In the other he carried the eternal lamp, using it to light his way into the forest. His steps took him to the carcass of the cockatrice.

He put the lamp down and then used his shovel to carefully scoop every cockatrice bone and ligament from

DANIEL ROY GREENFELD

the ground. Then he moved his right hand down the handle of the shovel to just before the blade, allowing him to hold it single-handed. With his left hand, he lifted the lamp and used it to guide his way out of the forest, back to the pyre.

He took his time going back. One misstep or simply brushing the spade of the shovel might bring him in contact with the carcass. A single touch would bring him down, and unlike Ram he wouldn't be brought to the healer in time to be saved.

Finally, he was back at the pyre. Bull had erected it next to the stream, including the stump as part of its construction. This would be far enough from the forest to not to risk the fire spreading.

Bull lowered the lamp, and then taking the shovel in two hands he lifted its lethal cargo above the wood. He turned the shovel, carefully placing its gruesome load into a crevice in the huge pile of logs. The broken remnants of the dead cockatrice mottled the timber with its still virulent poison. The scoop of the shovel was pitted and scarred. Having completed the most dangerous part of his labor, he tossed the shovel onto the logs for good measure.

Bull broke the seal on the jar of holy oil. He picked it up, knowing it was meant only for special occasions, praying that this was such a time. He poured it into the tinder, praying that it would be enough to ignite the still-green logs.

The Pyre   25

He looked down at his handiwork, the timbers, the tinder, and now the temple oil. All that remained was to light his handiwork: a funeral pyre that wasn't for the cockatrice, but for Ram, the son he had injured for life. For the wife he had hurt. For the man he had been.

Bull picked up a torch. He lit it with the eternal lamp. He stepped towards the pile of wood and paused.

His body hurt.

That was good.

He felt the aches in his muscles. The twinges in his joints. The blisters covering the palms of his hands. Tears dried on his cheeks. Hunger burned in his belly. His dry throat burned from working without pause to drink. This was penance.

Bull prayed aloud, his first spoken words since he had screamed at his wife. "Great Hyperion," he prayed, "please make this fire burn. Please. Let me avenge my son. Burn the cockatrice into ashes. Not for me, but to finally destroy this curse. Please. I beg you. Grant me this favor. For the sin of violating dryad law, when the priest or knight-magistrate come I will meekly accept any punishment. I will do any penance that they command."

Bull knew that the wood should be too green to burn. He trembled with anxiety because he knew it would take a miracle to light. Then he lit the oil-soaked tinder in several places. The tinder caught quickly. He backed away.

He watched with trepidation as the fire spread through the smaller branches. Would Hyperion strike him down for stealing from the temple? For chopping down a tree? Or did the king of the gods, the lord of fire and sun, bless his deeds? Without such a blessing, Bull knew full well that the just-chopped-down tree logs would not burn.

Quickly the fire grew, lighting the greater logs, turning into a bonfire. It blazed with such terrible heat that Bull had to back far away.

Hyperion had passed judgment.

CHAPTER 4

HEROES AND GOBLINS

Two years passed.

In the early evening of the first month of summer, five figures moved stealthily down the narrow street. They had to be careful. One wrong move and they would alert the enemy. They had just one chance to spring their trap, to best the foe and to save the world. Slowly, carefully, on their tiptoes, they made not a sound. Finally they were in position. They waited for just the right moment. Then they charged forward, shouting ancient war cries.

Five boys leapt from a narrow street into the village square. Brandishing sticks like swords, they slashed and cut at imaginary foes. Transformed through play into a world of legend, the center of the little town was now a vast battlefield, containing the endless ranks of fiendish goblins.

DANIEL ROY GREENFELD

Wren was now seven, though small for his age. Ram at eight was as big as a ten year old. Ram was no longer bright. He didn't talk much, but he liked to play with Wren. The long summer day meant that even after chores were finished and supper eaten, there was much time to play.

Since the accident, Ram and Wren had grown even closer together. Even when not told to do so, they always stuck together. In the children's sleeping loft, they slept next to each other. They helped each other with chores. Wren seemed to be able to read his older brother's mind. He often said things on his behalf. They had become inseparable, two halves of the same person.

When their chores were done, Wren and Ram loved to play at being heroes. Sometimes they were dryads casting mighty spells that raised magic tree castles and ships into the sky. They would shoot impossible targets with arrows or swing their imaginary magical swords. Other times they skipped around as if they were knights on horseback, decimating hordes of goblins. When they played in the mud, they were golems building mighty stone castles and firing booming guns that scared everything away. Wren loved these games. They made him feel big and strong.

Today, Wren and Ram were playing heroes with three boys who lived around the bend. Wren carried a stick that to his child's eye was a magic sword. With his sword, he was Turgon the Valiant, the hero who killed three Goblin Kings in one day! Riding a great white steed, Turgon led his army into glorious battle against the goblin hordes. His sword was Goblin's Bane, enchanted in the First or Second Age—Wren could never keep track of the Ages—and the goblins fell for it. Only the Goblin Kings had the strength to stand against him. For all their might, Turgon chopped off the heads of the three Goblin kings.

"Whack! Whack! Whack!" So went the "chopping off three Goblin King heads" chorus of the better song about Turgon the Valiant, the one they had learned at night over the hearth fire after dinner. The other song was long and boring and only traveling musicians knew all the words.

Ram was Swacker the Strong, chosen entirely because he laughed anytime someone said his name. He was a golem axe man, cut from black, lightly speckled granite so his skin looked like the starry sky. Swacker the Strong's axe was said to be as tall and heavy as a horse. Ram carried the biggest, heaviest fallen tree branch he could find! Against imaginary enemies he would slam it into the ground, causing the earth to shake like a drum. Then, he would pick up the monsters above his head and throw them down the well. When the boys would stop to get a drink from the well, Ram said the water was "monster beer" and all the boys in the game would pretend to be drunk.

This evening, along with the three other village boys, Wren and Ram flung themselves against the imaginary goblin horde. Countless goblins were crushed and broken! Next, the bigger hobgoblins fell before their mighty weapons. Then came a score of mighty drakontos, the brutish half-giants, and the battle was truly on. The heroes, outnumbered and outmatched, were bashed through the air, landing miles away.

The boys, their play matching the story, flung themselves through the air, only to land and roll across the ground until they were dizzy. Being dizzy was fun, so they would stand up and stagger around.

"Ram!" their mother shouted from the house. "Come here at once!"

Wren turned to Ram and saw the guilty look on his face. "Did you finish your chores?" Wren asked.

"No." Ram shook his head.

"We have to go," Wren said to the other boys.

Wren took Ram by the hand, and they walked home. Peony, their mother, scolded Ram. She swatted his bottom. Then she put him back to work.

Wren tried to help his brother, but his mother pushed him away. "Not this time. Ram can do his own chores. Go and play, Wren," she said.

For a moment Wren stood there, watching his brother. Then he noticed his little sister Protea looking at him hopefully. Not wanting to be forced to include her in his play, he ran away. He ran back to where the three other boys continued the game of heroes.

"Where's Ram?" asked Sparrow, at nine the oldest of the boys. In their game, he played Boru Strongbow.

"Chores," Wren answered.

"To the Tower of Sorcery!" shouted Ox, eight years old and playing Edalion Demon Slayer. He led the boys to the tree that had served in this role to generations of boys. Wren joined them, slipping into the world of heroes with the ease of a seven-year old.

Finch, Sparrow's younger brother, was Wren's age. He squatted in the dirt and drew a map. He knew all the lands and secret places, for he was Hallorean the Marchwarden. "There are goblins nearby, over by the Mountains of Despair," he said.

"That's not the Mountains of Despair!" Wren said. "That's my home!"

"Your home is the Mountains of Despair because goblins live there, and you're as small as a goblin," Finch declared with the assurance of Hallorean the Marchwarden.

"Wren is a goblin!" mocked Sparrow, taking advantage of the situation to tease the smallest boy.

"I am not!"

DANIEL ROY GREENFELD

"Wren is a goblin! Get him!"

Wren ran. Being the smallest, he was caught quickly by Ox and Sparrow. They grabbed him and made him fall down. They held him there, pinched him, called him goblin poo. When he cried out, Finch sat on his face and made obscene noises. Wren could barely breathe and struggled uselessly. Any of the other boys easily outweighed him.

Struggling under the weight of Finch and Sparrow, Wren heard running footsteps. Finch was shoved off, knocked sprawling to the ground. Then Sparrow was pulled off and dragged through the dirt.

It was Ram.

Ox got up, but not before getting in one last painful pinch. Then he ran to help Sparrow against Ram. Ram let go of Sparrow's arms and met Ox in a shoving match. Sparrow got up and joined in the shoving. Outnumbered, Ram still had the strength and determination to match them both.

Finch was up again. He ran up behind Ram and pulled him by his tunic. The struggle was now uneven. Ram would be bowled over in moments.

Wren jumped up and grabbed Finch, who let go of Ram. The two boys pulled each other for a moment.

Then Finch tripped Wren, landing on top of him. Finch rained blows down on Wren, who cried and screamed.

"Get off of him!" Ram shouted. His brother needed his help. He furiously drew on the power of Swacker the Strong. Like the golem had done against a drakontas, Ram stopped shoving and started pulling. Swinging the other boys around, they staggered into Wren and Finch. Finch screamed in pain as they fell over him.

"Stop! Stop! Stop!" Their parents ran in and broke up the fight.

"Goblins! Goblins!" Finch, Sparrow, and Ox taunted.

Ram tried to run at them, but he was restrained by the strong arms of his father, Bull. Wren wept and was comforted by their mother, Peony.

Peony and Bull took them home. As the sun set, Peony cleaned their scratches and scrapes. Assured that tomorrow would be another brighter day, Peony put Wren and Ram to bed.

Beneath the children's loft, their older siblings and parents talked quietly below.

Wren cried quietly. His eye hurt. His lip was swollen. Worse was how badly his pride was damaged. The memory of Finch sitting on his face was humiliating. Even when his brother had come to help, he had been useless.

"Don't cry," Ram said, attempting to soothe him. "I'll protect you. I'll always protect you."

Ram's soothing made it worse. It went against Wren's already injured pride. Ram had saved him, but when he tried to save Ram back, Finch had beaten him up. It meant that Ram thought Wren couldn't fend for himself. That was the worst. It was a terrible end to a terrible day.

Wren had to make it right. "Some day I'll save you back. I promise," he said.

CHAPTER 5

SECOND COMET

This year, once it grew dark, no one strayed outside the village walls.

It was another year that a comet visited the skies. Their parents said that this year the misfortune was not as bad as seven years ago when the last comet burned in the skies. But to Wren it was scary. With his own young eyes, he had seen goats and pigs producing misshapen offspring. More babies than usual were stillborn this year. The worst of it was the howling of the wolves and hissing of weald hounds late at night, but so far the beasts had troubled no one in Wren's village. The neighboring villages, on the other hand, had fended off several wolf attacks.

Ten and eleven years old respectively, Wren and Ram were given chores that reflected their maturity and independence. This meant for them that they became goat herders. Typically this task involved boys and girls

DANIEL ROY GREENFELD

taking their herds off in separate directions. Yet Wren and Ram always stayed together. Normally this might be frowned upon, but the comet had everyone looking after their own. No one minded that the two brothers watched out for each other.

It was late autumn, when most leaves had fallen and the air had that certain cold bite. There was still green growth below, so the goats ate away at the foliage at the edge of the forest. Keeping watch over them was tedious, so Wren and Ram practiced with their slings.

They used the overhand throw, releasing their stones near the top of the swing. This gave their stones a flat trajectory. Their target was the bole of an old tree. Wren's throws were about as accurate as his older brother's, but Ram's were extremely powerful for his age. In fact, one of his casts that went low struck a rock in the ground, shattering with a loud clatter and sending pieces flying everywhere.

One of the flying rock chips stung Wren in the forehead. He smacked his hand to his head and said, "Ouch! I got hit!"

"Sorry," Ram said. He grinned.

"You sling as hard as a hero," Wren said, complimenting his brother. Then, he turned a bit away from the target, his empty hand facing the tree. He knew that the trick was to turn his whole body while casting the sling, since that generated more velocity.

"The goats," Ram told Wren just as he was about to cast.

Wren stopped his windup. He looked where his brother was pointing. The goats were wandering off, going deeper into the woods. The brush was thicker there. It would be easy to lose one of their charges in the dense brush. The stupid beasts could wander deep into the woods, where things would prey on them.

Tucking their slings into pockets, the boys began to round up their combined herd. They were making good progress when Wren heard a plaintive bleat on the other side of the thorny bramble.

"I'll take care of it!" Wren said and began searching for a way past or through the bushes. He found a narrow pathway that would require some precision for him to cross. It took him a few minutes and cost him a few painful pricks, but he managed to get to the other side.

Wren saw the goat. It was trotting away from the bushes, following a girl with long red hair. She was about as tall as him. She was skipping away.

"Hey! That's my goat! Stop!" Wren shouted. He raced after her. She didn't even bother to turn to face him. Instead, she moved deeper and deeper into the trees and brush. He chased her between trees, over fallen limbs, down a slope, and into a clearing. She stopped in the sunlight and turned to face him, a little smile on her face.

He slowed to a walk and tried not to make his gasping obvious. She wasn't tired, but then again, he was always short of wind.

"You aren't from the village," he said. "Who are you?"

As he came closer, he noticed she was rather homely. Ugly even. All girls were gross, but she could win a contest at the fair for grossness. Her clothes were a mess, dirty and tattered.

"I'm hungry. Please let me keep the goat," she said, looking down. Her voice was odd, almost the trilling of a flute.

"What's your name?" he asked.

She smiled sadly and spoke in her curious piping voice. "You can call me Cora," she said.

"I'm Wren. I can't let you keep the goat," Wren said.

Her face fell.

"If you'd like, I can bring you to the village, and they'll give you a meal there."

"They would not like me in your village," Cora said, looking down at the ground.

"Why? Because you're an orphan?"

"I'm ugly and worse."

He shrugged. All girls were ugly. He took her by the hand and gently pulled her back the way they had come.

"Please don't make me go to the village," she begged. Yet she took a step along with him. He pulled a little harder, and she picked up her pace to match.

"It's not so hard, is it Cora?"

"This is the easy part. Later things will become very hard. You won't like me then."

Wren couldn't even conceive arguing with her about the liking part. Not only was she ugly, but she also smelled bad. Her clothes smelled like wet animal fur, her breath like a dog's. Her only saving grace was her rather lovely voice. That and maybe her long red hair, which was shinier than a horse's mane.

As they approached the bramble, he heard Ram calling from the other side. "Wren! Where are you?"

"I'm coming, and I'm bringing a guest!" Wren called back.

"I don't want to go," she pleaded.

"You must," he said.

She nodded tearfully and then followed him into the sticky path through the bramble. The branches brushed against their skin, piercing them with their thorns. Cora took the pain stoically. Wren did his best to copy her, taking care not to say "Ouch" as frequently as he usually did.

Ram took a look at her. "She's weird," he said.

Wren forced himself not to laugh. "Her name is Cora. I think she's an orphan. We're taking her home with us."

"Why isn't her name a flower?" Ram asked.

"I don't know, Ram," Wren said. He shrugged. "Does it matter? Let's go!"

Ram looked troubled. But he followed his younger brother's wishes as dutifully as he did every other time.

Wren and Ram herded the goats back to the village, through one of the gates. Cora followed Wren closely, looking at him worriedly. Periodically she asked again and again that they go back. Finally, Wren snapped.

"Don't ask anymore!" he said.

After that, Cora didn't say anything. Her eyes remained wild, almost rabid with worry.

As the two boys prodded the goats into the market square, things started to go wrong. A baby started to cry. A cat hissed. A dog snarled, baring its fangs. The villagers, well acquainted with all the local children, stared at Cora, as if she was something else besides a strange looking girl. Wren couldn't help but notice that their faces seemed less than curious, rather touched with hatred.

"I told you. They hate me. There will be trouble," Cora said miserably.

"Let's go home. Mama and Papa will know what to do," Wren said. His voice had confidence that he didn't feel.

Across the square and down their road they went, followed by a few of the more aggressive members of the small community, not the least of which was Pheasant the Bootmaker. He was a loud and boisterous man known for being the sort of person to trouble visitors to the village.

As they approached their home and shed, Ram saw that their mother was outside. She was hanging clothes with the help of Dandelion and Protea. They looked up as Wren, Ram, and Cora approached with the herd of goats.

Wren saw his mother gave a curt command to his big sister, Dandelion. The teenaged girl took young Protea firmly by the wrist and dragged her into the house, protesting. Their mother picked up her washboard, holding it almost as if it were a weapon.

It was the weirdest behavior he had ever seen in his family.

"Mama, we found an orphan girl!" Wren said proudly. The teachings of the gods promoted charity, and he was proud that he was going to help poor Cora.

"She's not a girl, Wren," his mother said, trembling.

"What?" Wren said. He looked at Cora. She was ugly and smelled foul, but she was a girl. "I don't understand."

"Ram. Wren. Leave her be and come here. Right now!" his mother ordered.

Ram hastened to obey. Wren stayed, confused and torn.

His mother's face turned wrathful. "Wren, if you don't come over here right now, I'll belt you until you're black and blue. And then I'll hand you over to your father!"

Wren decided the threat of a belting trumped staying next to Cora. He dropped her hand and hurried over.

When he reached their mother, she stood in front of them, protectively. She said, "I don't know what you are, but please don't hurt me or my family."

"I'm just hungry," Cora said. "So very hungry."

"Take whatever you want from the flock. Just let us go. Please," his mother begged.

"Mom! She's just an orphan girl!" Wren tried to explain. "She needs our help!"

"I wasn't going to hurt him. I just wanted to meet him. I'll just take a goat and go." Cora said. She trilled and to Wren's amazement the goats obediently separated, making a path in the middle of the flock. Cora walked between them, to the other side of the flock. With another trill a single goat began to follow her as she walked past the brave souls who had followed them down the street.

Wren was shocked. You couldn't just sing goats apart, and yet she had done just that. Wren noticed his mother was shaking, nervous tension rolling off her. Yet, he had to know.

"Cora, what are you?" he called.

She stopped in her tracks. Slowly, as if fighting something inside, she turned to face Wren, Ram and their mother. "I'm a monster, born in the year of the comet seven years ago."

Wren saw it then. Her eyes were too fierce, her mouth too wide, her long red hair too perfect, her clothes...her clothes weren't clothes. They were folds of dirty, furry

DANIEL ROY GREENFELD

skin. Her feet weren't dirt-covered shoes, but rather dinner-plate sized paws of a great clawed beast.

"You see me now as others do. I will leave now before things become very hard," she said, unhappily.

As she turned to walk back to the square and out the village gate, it happened. One of the braver souls, Pheasant the Grocer, who had followed them down the road, threw the apple core he had been gnawing on. It struck Cora in the face. Wren saw the other villagers reach for things that they were carrying, to throw and humiliate the monster.

As they did so, he saw something from Cora's back erupt and shoot backwards. It landed several feet from her, and to his horror he realized it was her hindquarters. She wasn't a girl. She was a clawed monster on four legs. Her tail was long and as thick as his father's wrist, ending with a spike-covered tail. Her body was as large as a wolf's, but much more muscular.

She didn't roar. Instead she sang a furious storm of anger more beautiful and terrible than any pounding drum. She leapt and pounced on the man who had struck her, knocking him down, jaws descending as he screamed. The villagers scattered, in their panic rushing into homes that were not theirs. The goats bolted in absolute panic, racing down the street, leaping into open windows, even vainly attempting to climb the wattle walls of the village houses.

Wren felt himself being pulled into his family home. His last view of Cora was her bloody jaws opening so wide that he could see the extra rows of teeth. One great paw held down the headless corpse of Pheasant.

Then Wren's mother dragged inside his home. She slammed the door shut and fastened it with a thick wooden plank.

Screams and shouts filled their air for several minutes, followed by the sobbing of Wren's mother and siblings. Wren felt sadness. All Cora had wanted was something to eat. Never did she threaten anything. He had made her come, and things had gone dreadfully wrong.

CHAPTER 6

KNIGHT AND MONSTER

That night, while in the children's loft, Wren heard horses come down the street. The sound of hooves striking the stones grew louder as they approached. He could hear the jingle of harness as the horses were reined in to stop at his home's door. The unmistakable clatter of at least one man in armor dismounting heralded that whoever approached was important. Then, after all the other noise, there was an authoritative knock on the door.

Wren watched from the children's loft as his father took his great-grandpa's spearhead from its place above the hearth fire. Never rusting, never tarnished, even without its haft it would make a wickedly deadly short weapon. Wren had never been allowed to touch it, but he had seen the single mystical rune that lay on its leaf-shaped blade.

His father, Bull, a big man, moved carefully to the door, as if the door were going to burst in. "Who is it?" he asked.

"Your lord and magistrate, Sir Aethel, would have a word," said a strong, gravelly voice.

Bull opened the door. "Your honor," he said. He bowed deeply at the waist.

"I would speak to your wife and sons. May I come in?"

Bull backed up, allowing the knight to come in. Sir Aethel was a tall man, as tall as Wren's father. Like Bull, he was heavy in the chest, but with a rider's straight back. He wore a green and white checkered surcoat over carefully polished armor. The metal plates of his armor slid back and forth over each other as he walked and moved. If this armor was heavy, it was hard to tell because he moved lightly on his feet. He had taken off his helmet, revealing a shock of reddish-blond hair above a slightly homely face just past its youth. On his belt, his ancient magical sword was buckled. Many generations ago, the dryads had given it to his family for their service.

Sir Aethel nodded at Wren's mother, who gave him her best and deepest curtsey. Quietly but commandingly, he said, "Tell me what happened, Goodwife Peony."

She hesitated, and then Sir Aethel said more comfortably, "There will be no punishment. You and your family did nothing wrong."

"My two youngest sons were out herding goats beyond the wall. One of them found that thing. He brought it home with them. I begged it to leave. At first, it seemed ready to go. Then, it became angry and started killing. We ran inside and haven't left ever since."

"What did it look like?" Sir Aethel asked.

"At first like a terrible mockery of a little girl with long, red hair. Its voice wasn't natural. It had a foul-smelling tongue. When it became angry, it became huge. It grew extra legs and a tail with spikes. The head? The head never changed except to sniff the air like a serpent. A forked tongue it had, the same as a snake."

Wren was shocked. Tongue? What tongue? As far as Wren had seen, Cora might not even have a tongue! He wanted to say something, but he knew better than to interrupt.

"Did it eat anyone?" Sir Aethel asked.

"Your honor, I saw it bite the head off Pheasant the Grocer," Peony said. "He was just standing there minding his own business, and it leapt upon him biting. It was the most horrible thing I ever did see."

Wren knew this wasn't true. The grocer had been killed because he threw an apple core at Cora. Who wouldn't be upset with that kind of treatment?

The knight asked a few more questions, which Wren's mother answered with some embellishment. Wren knew she was getting a lot of the details wrong.

"May I talk to the boys who found the monster?" Sir Aethel asked, more of a command than a request. As soon as Wren heard his father say yes, he was hurtling down the ladder to the floor. Ram followed moments later.

Sir Aethel looked him over. Then he asked with a gentle voice, "Did you find the monster?"

"Yes," Wren said. "Her name is Cora. She never threatened anyone! She reacted when Pheasant the Grocer threw old fruit at her!" Wren explained as fast as he could.

"I see." The knight seemed tense. Wren didn't know why.

Then the knight demanded, almost angrily, "Where did you find it?"

Wren gulped, noticing that Sir Aethel called Cora an "it," not "her." "I found Cora just inside some of the brambles," Wren said. "One of our goats was following her. I thought she was just a lost girl, maybe from another village. I didn't know she was a monster. She seemed kind of nice."

The knight relaxed then. He tousled Wren's hair. "We live in an old world filled with many monsters. Some of them prey on our fears, desires, and even charity. Fortunately, we can guard ourselves with faith in the gods, faith in our overlords."

"Tomorrow, Wren, you will guide me and my men to where you found this 'Cora.' We'll bring tracking dogs to help us corner our prey. Then with the sword of my father's father's father, I will kill it."

"B-but she's just a girl," Wren protested.

"She's a man-eating monster!" shouted Sir Aethel. Wren cringed, as did his family. The knight, even for his station rather kindly, softened his voice, "Your sense of charity does you well, stripling. However, the monster has preyed on you like it would prey on any other victim."

"Milord, do you know what kind of monster it is?" asked Bull timidly.

"I'm pretty certain I do," Sir Aethel said. "By all descriptions, it has a body like a thinly red-furred muscular wolf, almost akin to the descriptions I have heard of lions. Yet its tail has spikes. Its head has the mane of a lion, yet it wears the face of a monstrous person. The rows of teeth lend another clue, as does its voice. In fact, it would be a perfect match for a *manticore* if it had wings."

"The minstrels tell stories about such things," Wren's mother said. She looked very worried. "They say they are man-eaters."

"Yes, they are. In fact, while I'm no scholar," Sir Aethel admitted, "I know that 'manticore' literally means 'man-eater.' The truth of a common minstrel's story isn't worth a damn, but in this I suspect they are correct. The monster, if it hasn't preyed on you yet, will begin to do so."

Wren felt a shock of fear. Had Cora been playing with him the way that a cat played with a mouse? If so, why did she accompany him into the village? The other thing was that she seemed kind of small to be a man-eating monster. She claimed to have been born in the year of the previous comet, just seven years ago. Could she be a young monster?

"I'll be back at morning's first light," Sir Aethel said. He walked to the door.

"I think she's just a young manticore," Wren said. "She told me she was born in the year of the comet. Perhaps she can be saved? Brought to the gods even?"

The knight stopped at the door and responded without turning back. "Anything monstrous that's born under a comet is too dangerous to live, boy. A young wolf is as cute as a dog puppy, but the adults will rip your heart out. Except this beast might grow wings and eat entire families! Parents, children, even babies! It's vile. If it's young, it's going to be easier to kill."

The knight walked out the door. Wren wanted to say something else. He opened his mouth to speak, but his mother grabbed him and clapped her hand over his mouth.

In the morning, Wren led Sir Aethel, two of his sergeants, and a huntsman leading a pair of dogs to the bramble where he had discovered Cora. They went into the woods while Wren's father walked him home. The villagers closed the gates and waited. For a day and a night, the sounds of the hunt could be heard from the forest. Dogs bayed and horns blared. Then came the battle, filling the air with roaring and screaming.

Near dusk, the temple bell was rung. Villagers assembled dutifully in the market square. On the steps of the temple, Sir Aethel stood, exhausted. His armor was battered. In his right hand, he carried his ancestral rune sword. In his left hand, he dragged a bloody bag.

When Wren saw the bag, he trembled. He wondered why Cora had followed and listened to him. Why would she have done that? It made no sense.

"Thanks to the grace of the gods, the manticore is no more!" Sir Aethel said, raising the bag with its grisly contents to the sky. The villagers cheered to the stars.

"From this day hence, you will not be plagued with the manticore's evil! The hunger! The deceptions!" said Sir Aethel.

"Praise the gods!" Wren's mother shouted, a call that was picked up by others.

Sir Aethel didn't pause. "The monster pleaded for its life. It said that it was sent to protect you. This is a lie! It lied to me, and I know it lied to you. Whatever deceptions the monster told you are false. Forget them! It was an agent of the Adversary, sent to harm you. Nothing more! I am your protector. I will protect you now and until the end of my days!"

The people of the village cheered. Even Ram cheered. Beer and applejack were brought out. The villagers celebrated, raising their mugs to toast. Sir Aethel maintained his decorum but accepted a hefty mug of brew as a courtesy. Musical instruments appeared. The drinking led to dancing and even more fun.

Wren never felt more alone in his life.

The very next day, wolves began to strike the village of Perswald. They came in the morning, and they came in the night. Lone travelers vanished. Livestock were eaten. It was the first time that wolves had come since the comet arrived ten months ago

Wren might have felt vindication, but the work of a goat herder became much harder. He and Ram had to move the livestock carefully to the edge of the woods. They placed them on staked leashes and then allowed them to crop the brush.

Cora's death had removed an unknown protector. No one thought of her this way but Wren.

CHAPTER 7

COOKING POT

Like the other gobs and hobs, Abrog dug around in the dirt near the stream and the brambles. He had figured out that a stick could break up the hard parts of the ground.

He was so hungry! He couldn't wait, so he dug frantically into the dirt. He hoped to find a chewable root, worm, insect, or anything in the ground that he could shove into his mouth. He wasn't at the point of gnawing tree bark again, but he wasn't far from it.

Abrog, like most young gobs, was small and spindly. His green skin was still covered with the soft, grey fur of the very young of his kind. His face was soft and smooth. Sharp rows of teeth filled his mouth, for gobs needed frequent replacements for lost teeth. Less than a year since his hatching, he was the size of a human toddler, except agile and quick. Able to eat anything, whether

DANIEL ROY GREENFELD

insect, root, or tree bark, he was fully capable of feeding himself.

Gobs and hobs were children goblins and hobgoblins, uncared for by anyone, left to fend for themselves since hatching from eggs buried in shallow ground.

What Abrog really craved was the meat eaten by the goblins and hobgoblins. Even if that meat was stewed gob or hob, their meals smelled savory and filling.

Abrog was starving, but he dared not steal their food. Stealing from adults was dangerous. Being caught usually meant being doomed to the cooking pot. If he survived, he would be fully grown within two years. Then he would finally be able to eat stew with the adults. Such was the way that goblin kind treated their young.

Abrog's digging partner was his clutch-mate and sister Orbag. Like her brother, she had soft-grey fur, but her skin was red, not green. About the same height as her brother, her joints were thicker, her spine straighter. She would grow larger and taller than her brother, causing a sundering of the strong familial bond of youth. They had always been together for as long as they could remember, which wasn't very long. Being children, their vocabulary was quite small, yet, instinctively they knew each other well. Orbag was the better smeller, good at finding things in the ground. She fended off the other gobs and hobs from stealing their food. Abrog was very good at sneaking. He was also the better listener.

Indeed, his pointed ears caught a noise above them. Abrog darted to the side. He squealed a warning. A full-grown goblin dropped from a branch above them, landing where he had just been squatting.

Orbag didn't have a chance. The goblin scooped her up in his hunting blanket. With practiced movements, he tied a knot to prevent her from escaping. She squealed in fear. The blanket shook violently with her futile efforts to escape.

The other gobs and hobs around Abrog darted into the nearby brambles, able to dodge the sharp thorns with ease. The adult goblin, nearly five times his height, blocked Abrog's path to safety. Left no choice, Abrog ran in the other direction.

"I'm sorry," apologized the goblin as it gave chase. "But the hobgoblins will give me a hiding if I don't provide them meat today."

Abrog ran toward the stream. This was unfortunate, for the stream had carved a deep channel through the forest. Even for the adult goblins and hobgoblins, it was not an easy barrier to cross. Nevertheless, empowered by fear, little Abrog ran faster than he ever had before. Once he got to the stream, there was nowhere to go, so he simply jumped off the bank. The fall, twice the height of a hobgoblin might kill him, but he didn't want to be another screaming gob tossed into the cooking pot.

He had aimed for the rocky bank on the other side of the stream. Landing so hard on those stones would certainly leave his body shattered and broken. For a moment, Abrog wondered if it had been a mistake to run this direction. Then he remembered his pursuer.

Unable to propel himself to the rocky shore on the other side with his little legs, Abrog landed in the fast-flowing stream. He went in over his head, plunging into the water. Then he bobbed to the surface. Quickly the current carried him away.

"Well done, little one," said the big goblin as Abrog was swept away. "Gorgol hopes you grow up and join the hunters!"

Abrog barely noticed as he struggled to stay alive. He had never swum before. Even if he had, the rocks and rapids of the fast-flowing stream tossed him back and forth in the water violently. He was dreadfully aware that his head or body could be smashed against a rock, potentially leaving his body for scavengers or the cooking pot.

The stream turned a bend. The rushing current pushed him into the dangling roots of a tree at the edge of the river. He grabbed them and held on desperately, his rows of teeth chattering.

Feeling the cold water draining his strength, Abrog pulled himself deeper into the roots. There, he found a dry space carved by previous floods. He rested there for some time.

He cried. He missed Orbag. Along with the sadness, deep inside he felt boiling rage and frustration that she had been taken for the pot. He wished he could have protected her, or struck back at Gorgol. He wished he wasn't here in the roots, but rescuing his sister before she was thrown into the cooking pot.

Abrog felt the inadequacy of youth and gender. Being so young, adulthood seemed forever in the future, even if it was just two years away. Even when he grew up, he would just be a male, smaller and weaker than the female hobgoblins.

"No more crying," Abrog shouted, sitting up. "Gorgol, I'll get you back for taking Orbag away, I'll get the hobgoblins back for eating my sister. I don't know how or when, but I promise that Orbag will be avenged. I'll make it so that gobs and hobs won't be food for grown ups. This I swear. I swear it by the moon, the stars, even the accursed sun."

Abrog shook with fury and determination, the chill and hunger forgotten. He pounded the roots with his little fists until the spell passed. He took in a great shuddering breath and was still.

Thinking of Orbag, he sniffed the air. It smelled of water and musty roots. But there was something else.

In the clay wall of the dry space, he smelled something unusual. Something that smelled strangely like food. He poked at the soft clay with a claw several times until it clicked against something. That click sounded different than tapping a rock. Using his little clawed fingers, he dug frantically. It took a long time, but eventually he pried and dragged the strange-smelling object out of the wall.

It was a chest about half his size. He knew what a chest was because the chieftain had much bigger chests containing the wealth of the tribe. Unlike the rotting containers of the tribe, this seemed in perfect condition. In fact, the sticky clay fell off as he examined it, and in minutes it was unbelievably clean.

Etched into the wood were weird lines and a face that wasn't of goblin stock. It was elongated with clean lines. The only similarity with goblins that Abrog could identify was the pointed ears. Even those were longer than a goblin's. He touched his own ears, so uncommonly long for any gob.

From stories told by the hobgoblins and goblins at the cooking fire, he thought that the face might belong to a dryad. Well, the dryad wasn't here. Finders, keepers.

There wasn't a padlock on the chest, so Abrog opened his find.

Inside were packages each bigger than his fist, wrapped in leaves. They smelled of the foulest food. Abrog nearly gagged on the stench.

His belly growled. He didn't care how awful the food tasted. He needed to eat!

He unwrapped one of the packages revealing a cake made from nuts, berries, honey, and a terrible combination of herbs that smelled wretched. The cake felt oddly hot in his hands, and he broke off a gob-sized bite from one of the corners. He popped it in his mouth and chewed.

He gagged. It was the worst thing ever! If it weren't for his hunger, he would have spat it out. He swallowed it and regretted it instantly as it burned down his gullet.

Seeking relief, Abrog crawled over to the water's edge. He put his face into the water and drank the cooling water. That eased the pain. He came up for air. Then he went down for another long drink.

The burning had turned into a nice warm feeling. He felt extremely tired. He crawled over to the wall, sprawled next to the chest, and was fast asleep.

CHAPTER 8

BONES AND STONES

Abrog and Gorgol squatted in the dirt over their playing board, a grid scratched into the hard earth. Filling a clearing in the forest, a score of goblins, gobs, and hobs crowded around the players. This was a much-anticipated game. They had waited until the full moon to play in the bright moonlight.

The reigning champion, Gorgol, was known to be unbeatable at Bones and Stones. Having never lost a match in his adult years, he brimmed with confidence. "You're wasting your time challenging me, youngling," he said. "Gorgol does not lose!" The goblins watching jeered and threw jagged rocks at young Abrog.

Gorgol was also known as the tribe's best hunter. Respected by every goblin, he wore the animal skins from the tribe's latest catch, smelling strongly of putrid animal flesh. Other goblins wore older skins that had worn out their odors. On his head was his fox head hat, its fangs drooping over Gorgol's forehead.

Gorgol's challenger, Abrog, was now a yearling gobber. Ahead of his peers mentally and physically, no other yearling could beat him at Bones and Stones. Abrog had already challenged some of the adult goblins earlier, beating them easily.

As he had grown toward adulthood in the past year, Abrog had become the smartest of the yearlings. He had the intelligence to make plans, and he had been the first one to learn how to count, all because of the special cakes that he had found. His memory was also greatly enhanced.

It was unclear whether Gorgol remembered his opponent from a year ago, when he had caught Orbag and chased Abrog into a stream. Abrog remembered Gorgol clearly. He remembered his promise, but made no mention of it.

Tonight Gorgol and Abrog hunched over the playing board. Small bones and stones served as playing pieces. Each time a bone was captured, the responsible player could gnaw on the bone, as per the game's tradition. Remaining bones would be stashed away for later games or gnawing.

Abrog always stashed his bones away for later. Since he had started eating the cakes he had found, he didn't feel much desire to eat the normal goblin fare. He often pretended to scavenge and eat because he didn't want anyone poking around him, possibly discovering the secret cave where he stored the special cakes.

Abrog had observed Gorgol's play before this game. Other goblins, being not so bright, tended to charge their pieces directly across the board's center. In contrast, the canny hunter would defend with a few sacrificial pieces, which were quickly gobbled up. While the other player was cackling with triumph over scoring a few pieces from the talented hunter, Gorgol attacked from the sides. The other player, his pieces now in a poor defensive position, would find themselves quickly losing pieces and the game. Most goblins, with their short memories and reckless nature, fell again and again to Gorgol's tactics.

The attack Abrog now mounted was similar to the attacks of other goblins. However, instead of rushing pieces forward to capture Gorgol's sacrifices, Abrog kept his force together in one big clump. This slowed down his advance. The goblins around him hooted and jeered at his hesitancy. As Abrog predicted, Gorgol spread his pieces to the sides of the board, splitting them in two. His tactic remained valid, even with Abrog's slightly unusual play. Soon Gorgol would begin to attack from both sides.

"What, too scared of me to attack?" Gorgol taunted. The hunter cackled, confident that the usual battle of attrition would soon begin.

Abrog grunted. Having played hundreds of games against himself in the darkness of the cave, he was eager to finally try his strategy against Gorgol in a real game. In preparation for this match, he had imitated Gorgol's tactics over and over and found a weakness.

Gorgol had now completely split his forces. It was time for Abrog to make his play. He began moving his pieces to the left side of the board—all his pieces. Since he had advanced slowly, he was not quite at the dangerous center point of the board. That was where Gorgol could easily attack from both sides. In fact, it would take an extra turn for any of the other half of Gorgol's pieces to counter. Abrog's bones and stones, outnumbering Gorgol's halved force on the left, captured all of them quickly.

As Abrog captured Gorgol's pieces, the audience around became louder and louder. By the time Gorgol assembled his other half into position to attack, Abrog had a winning advantage in pieces. It was a decisive victory.

Take that! You take my sister away? I take away your pride, your respect, Abrog thought.

The gobbers and hobbers jumped and shouted at Gorgol's comeuppance. The goblins jeered at Gorgol, mocking him for losing to the youngster. Abrog stood up and grinned in the fang-filled way of yearlings.

Unhappy with losing to a grinning yearling, Gorgol screeched in fury and was upon him. Abrog tried to run away but ran into the spectators. Gorgol, older and still larger, picked him up and dropped him on the remaining pieces of the board. Then he began to punch and kick the stunned yearling. Abrog curled into a ball.

"Oww! Stop! That's enough! I got lucky!" Abrog cried. But Gorgol continued to kick.

After a minute, Gorgol stopped beating and panted. Then he took out his knife, reached down, and cut away the strap of Abrog's well-filled stash of gnawing bones.

"I'm taking your stash," Gorgol said, snarling. Then he kicked Abrog one more time. "That's for not respecting your elders," he said.

He stomped away. The other goblins drifted away from Abrog who lay there for a few minutes. Sniffling, he shakily got to his feet.

CHAPTER 9

THE CHALLENGE

"Ta-dum! Ta-dum! TA-DUM!" That was the tribe's drum, calling for assembly.

Limping from his beating, Abrog followed the other goblins through the trees. In front of them was a clearing dominated by a single, rocky hill. At its foot, a hobgoblin was beating on a great drum, made of a wooden barrel over which cowskin was stretched. Behind her was a cave entrance, from which sooty smoke emerged. This was the hearth of the tribe, the home of the hobgoblins. From here, the hobgoblins took their mates and the greatest of them ruled as chieftain.

Abrog walked past the pounding drum, entering the cave. At the entrance, the cave was rough-hewn like the little cave that dotted the stream. Further inside, the ground, walls, and ceiling became more even, like a tunnel. They were as even as goblin pickaxe and claw

DANIEL ROY GREENFELD

could make it, at least. The tunnel descended into the earth.

Abrog coughed as he breathed in the acrid, foul-smelling smoke that filled the tunnels. When he was little, this smoke had smelled delicious and wonderful, but the changes wrought on him by the cakes made it smell ugly and foul.

Like the others, he ignored the side passages. This was the domain of the hobgoblins; going off the beaten path was certain death. Finally he entered the great cave, already occupied by much of the tribe. Here the tribe's great cooking pot rested under a narrow hole in the ceiling. The hole was so small that the smoking of the cooking fire filled this room.

In the old days, the tribe's numbers had once been so great that they were uncountable. During gatherings, goblins and hobgoblins would crowd in the main room of the cave, spilling out into the connecting passages and side rooms. Now, even with most of the goblins and hobgoblins of the tribe present, the subterranean room was half empty.

Nevertheless, the sounds of chattering snarls and hooting cries filled the room with a deafening ruckus.

"SILENCE!" roared the chieftain. Her voice echoed through the cave.

She was Izog, mighty chieftain, terrible to her enemies, eater of the young, strongest of the tribe. There were hobgoblins taller and heavier, but none matched her for sheer power. From her broad shoulders hung plates of armor taken from the battlefield. Draped across her back was a bear cloak taken from the previous chieftain's corpse. Her tread was proud, arrogant in the knowledge that she was the toughest warrior in the tribe. Her boots had iron plates on the front to protect her from sneaky underlings, as well as to make her kicks more vicious. Her hands were big, powerful, and clawed. One hand held a thick, heavy chopping sword called a falchion. Her hairless, blocky head was much higher than that of any goblin, pock marked and scarred from countless fights. One pointed ear was gone, torn off in a duel. Her nose was flattened from a forgotten fistfight.

Chieftain Izog's face was blemished and battered. She reeked of decay, her teeth being a filthy morass. She was stupid, taking the most idiotic of advice, or punishing messengers for any bad news.

The goblins were terrified, yet they were thrilled to see her. Even if she was murderously dangerous, she was the most attractive female in the tribe. Mating with her often meant death. Izog was infamous for crushing ribs, strangling necks, or simply biting out the throats of the one she chose to quicken her eggs. Instinct was instinct, though. Rare was the goblin that could resist her call. However, Abrog found her repulsive.

DANIEL ROY GREENFELD

"Attention!" At Chieftain Izog's shouted command, the assembled goblins and hobgoblins quieted.

"Tomorrow night we attack Radnag's filthy tribe using the stream as our path. Everyone goes except the cook!" Izog declared.

The cave filled with the noise of dismay as the goblins all made their voices heard. It was a poor way to attack Radnag. Tomorrow night was the first full moon. They would be easily seen. The stream would also be a death trap, forcing the goblins together into one easy target. Worst of all, the stream faced Radnag's lair, meaning they would be running directly into her tribe's strongest defense. A lot of goblins wouldn't make it home.

"SILENCE!" roared Izog again in her bass voice. "I said SILENCE!"

Unhappily, the goblins brought their complaints to a low murmur.

"Yes, it is an unusual way to attack," Izog declared, "but our fortune teller, Lurtz, assures me of victory!"

The goblins rose and cheered. Lurtz was a goblin like them, but one who had done well. In the eyes of the others, Lurtz was a true fortune teller and an asset. If asked, he would list all his accurate predictions. He correctly anticipated the rains, the snows, when other tribes would attack, and more.

Most goblins were skinny, bony, appearing almost at the edge of starvation. Lurtz was the exception. So well did he live that he was the rarity, a fat goblin. Sitting at the chieftain's side, he ate his fill from the cooking pot at every meal. He also rarely ventured outside, enjoying the fruits of other goblin's labor. His face was chubby, of a pale, unhealthy shade of green covered with warts. He wore a real cloth robe that he declared best suited his needs as a fortune teller, but its real purpose was to hide the growing belly that marked his sloth. Yet the goblins admired this belly, for it meant that he prospered. Unlike other goblins who risked their lives during mating seasons, Lurtz had high enough status with the chieftain to enjoy safe breeding.

From the rolls of fat that were his neck dangled necklaces made of the knucklebones of goblins, men, and bears in what he declared matched the placement of the stars in the sky. His club was adorned with bird feathers and pretty river stones. Both the necklaces and club were a critical tool in his predictions.

Lurtz's talent for fortune telling was a farce. He would make predictions, and then no matter what happened, he would change his story to match. After any important thing happened, he would declare another correct prediction. Anyone who contested Lurtz's declarations could not match the fortune teller's wily tongue.

So adept was Lurtz at his lies that he had completely convinced Izog of his value and had been appointed First Goblin. This role was always appointed to the

DANIEL ROY GREENFELD

smartest goblin of the tribe. Of the goblins, only Abrog had figured out Lurtz's lies and schemes.

The planned attack was as stupid as a frontal attack in Bones and Stones against Gorgol. It would fail, and lots of Abrog's tribe mates would die from arrows and javelins before Izog ran away.

The problem for yearling Abrog was that yearlings were always corralled into the front of attacks. While large for a goblin his age, he had no illusions about his chances of surviving the evening. Flight would be impossible, for Izog would send Gorgol and the other hunters to track him down.

To survive, Abrog knew that he had to contest Lurtz's predictions and reveal him as a fraud. It was dangerous, because again he would have to contest with a superior. If he failed, Lurtz would surely convince Izog that Abrog belonged in the cooking pot. He had seen it before when goblins had opposed the deceitful fortune teller. If he succeeded, he would face the ire of the fortune teller. This meant that he would have to beat Lurtz in such a way that Izog would recognize Lurtz' incompetence.

A plan leaped into Abrog's head. He had to act quickly before Izog commanded the tribe to march. He pushed forward out of the crowd, pointed a clawed finger at Lurtz and shouted in his high-pitched yearling's voice, "Deceitful liar! His predictions are false!"

The crowd went silent. Even Izog could not make them this quiet.

"You dare?!" screamed Lurtz, who stomped forward. He raised his club high, divining knucklebones clattered on his chest.

"Your fortunes are lies! Smashing me doesn't change that!" Abrog yelled, backing up. Lurtz followed, murder in his eyes.

"HOLD!" Izog commanded in her big voice. Lurtz froze in his tracks and turned to Izog in disbelief. Izog smiled with confidence at her fortune-teller. "The yearling merely wants to escape the front rank. He will not. Unleash your divinations on him and end this farce."

"Of course, my chieftain," Lurtz said in his silky voice. "I predict this one will die tonight at the hands of Radnag's tribe."

Before the predictions could go any further, Abrog executed the first step in his plan. He shouted quickly, "If your powers are real, then fortune tell yourself a victory in a game of Bones and Stones!"

Lurtz hesitated for a second. Then he laughed. Abrog had never seen him play a game. He suspected the reason Lurtz didn't play games was that losing would undermine his position as a fortune teller. Abrog desperately hoped that his youth would tempt Lurtz into accepting a game challenge.

DANIEL ROY GREENFELD

"I will predict your every move," Lurtz declared. "When you lose, I shall see to it personally that you stay in the front rank."

Abrog put fear into his eyes but smiled inside. He had been very pleasantly surprised on how easy it was to defeat Gorgol. Indeed, he was confident he would crush Lurtz. Lurtz' lack of divinatory ability meant that there was no way that the older goblin could know how good Abrog had become, much less predict his moves.

The board was drawn. Since Lurtz didn't usually play, he didn't even have a stash of playing pieces. Chieftain Izog lent him pieces from her own stash. As Abrog lowered his hand to the bag that held his own stash, he realized the flaw in his plan.

Gorgol had taken his stash.

Abrog despaired. He would be in the front ranks. He would die tonight.

"You dropped something," a voice said. Abrog turned. Gorgol stood there holding Abrog's pouch. He handed the bag to the yearling and whispered in his ear, "I don't want Lurtz's stupid plan to kill me. I'm counting on you to save us from it."

The match was on.

From the first move, Abrog knew he had won. Lurtz moved his pieces in a straight battle line across the board. In opposition, Abrog played Gorgol's game, keeping token pieces in the center near his side while splitting his forces to either side. He likened this strategy to the horns of a bull. Lurtz tried to maintain his line. Yet under the pressure of Abrog's side forces and intent on taking the apparently weak central defense, Lurtz battle-line bulged forward.

At the critical point, when pieces in the center were being captured in a slow battle of attrition, Abrog brought his side forces together. His "bull horns" consumed the edges of Lurtz's flank. Encircled by the yearling's attack, Lurtz desperately tried to defend, but the game was effectively over.

Izog, who stood by the board, recognized when Abrog had decided the game.

"The yearling has beaten you!" she roared, turning on Lurtz. Raising her falchion, she asked, "How could you not win? Where are your fortunes?"

For a moment, Lurtz was at a loss for words. That was too long for Izog, who took the fortune teller's head off. Splattered with goblin ichor and shocked by the sudden violence, Abrog forgot to flinch or run.

"Tell me, little one," Izog said, looking down at Abrog, "Tell me about the plan advised by Lurtz."

Abrog took a deep breath and said, "It is as stupid as I am small. No amount of luck or fortune could make it work."

Izog grinned, her mouth full of fangs and tusks. "This little one is smart. He will replace Lurtz as First Goblin," she said.

CHAPTER 10

CHIEFTAIN

A year later and fully grown into an adult goblin, Abrog lowered himself by the roots of the tree that still hung into the stream. His feet dangling just above the water, he swung from root to root using just his hands until he landed in his cave. This trick was easy. His arms were long, laced with corded muscle.

He picked up and opened the shiny magic chest. Hungry, he pulled out the last morsel of the cakes he had found, which he had lived on for the past year. So unbelievably filling a bite of these cakes would sate his hunger for days. He hadn't scrounged in the dirt since that fateful day, instead growing up on his hidden cache. He had kept it secret by only visiting it during the day, which was when the tribe slept. Goblin kind, being nocturnal, saw better at night than during the day. Even those that were awake had trouble seeing.

DANIEL ROY GREENFELD

Since he had begun eating the cakes he had noticed a fog lifting from his mind. He simply outsmarted every other gob, hob, yearling, and goblin, to the point that the Chieftain had made him First Goblin when he was still a yearling. He could tell when arguments were brewing, or when treachery was afoot. He could win at any game, but he made a point of losing to hobgoblins, as winners of smaller stature risked beatings and worse.

Not that his stature was lacking anymore. His limbs remained spindly compared to hobgoblins, but when standing straight he was the height of most hobgoblins. The patchwork armor he wore didn't weigh him down like it did the other young goblins. His axe felt as light as a feather, and he could swish it like a light branch. Rather than display his physical talents, his heightened intellect cautioned him to hide his size, so he affected a bent-over posture much more pronounced than any other goblin.

He put the last bite into his mouth, relishing the delicious mix of seeds, grains, honey, and bitter herbs that once repulsed him. As he chewed, he felt a familiar rush of power through his limbs. He knew that this would not last more than an hour, but that would be enough. Right now he felt like he could take on the world.

He climbed out of his hole, pausing to look down into the slowly moving water. The image that stared back at him was so different from any other goblin that he knew. The skin of his face was as smooth as a gob's, unblemished by wart or rash. His cheekbones were more angular than any other goblin, his jaw pointed like the face on the box that had contained the cakes, his nose straight and pointed. His eyes were dark and brooding.

Abrog looked away, finishing his climb. He stalked his way back to the hole in the side of the hill, the cave that was the center point of the tribe.

The hunting had been good recently, so the cave was filled with his kind, goblins chattering and squabbling with hobgoblins towering over them. The bigger or tougher you were, the more status you had. The hobgoblins took advantage of their size to lord over their smaller mates, the goblins.

Tonight, Abrog resolved, that was going to change.

In the center of the great cave, Izog the hobgoblin chieftain and the other hobgoblins sat in front of the giant cooking pot. They waited as the goblin cook stirred whatever or whomever had been unfortunate enough to be tossed in. His sister Orbag had certainly ended her short existence in this pot about two years ago.

Abrog walked up to the chieftain. She lounged on a bundle of dirty furs on a rock chipped into a rough throne facing the cooking pot. Instead of cowering low in fear as he had done before, he bared his fangs, axe, and shield. Boldly he shouted, "Izog, I challenge!"

DANIEL ROY GREENFELD

The raucous noise of the tribe came to a halt. A challenge meant control of the tribe for the winner and the cooking pot for the loser.

"Someone kill this too-smart runt for me!" snarled chieftain Izog.

The biggest hobgoblin, the hulking yet loyal Skoldoh, rose to her feet to defend Izog. Skoldoh was even larger than Izog, and preferred a massive war maul. While not as unpredictable as Izog, she would hurt and maim the smaller of the tribe. Unlike the goblins, she fed well, both on prey and on those who went into the pot. The goblins were rightly terrified of beasts like Skoldoh. In fact, Abrog knew Skoldoh relished a bit of lethal exercise now and then.

However, Abrog wasn't afraid anymore.

Before she could ready herself, Abrog moved with sudden, blazing speed. He kicked Skoldoh in the face. Abrog lifted his knee up high and attempted to put the sole of his boot through the back of his target's skull. Skoldoh flew off her feet and landed on the stone floor, the back of her head striking the ground with a loud crack. She lay very still. Blood started to pool underneath her skull.

Abrog had killed his first hobgoblin.

Abrog straightened to his full height. He felt the bones in his spine crack in relief. He towered over the goblins and easily matched the height of the hobgoblins.

"So afraid you are of little Abrog," he taunted the chieftain, with the high voice of a gob. Then his short life's worth of anguish and torment fed that voice. The venom of his life spilled out in a deafening bass roar, "Now fear Abrog, who will kill you and feast on your bones!"

The entire tribe flinched, including Izog. Everyone saw the chieftain blanch for a moment. The assembled hobgoblins and goblins whispered. Abrog grinned. Izog's sideways glances meant that she knew they had seen her moment of fear. The chieftain roared and leapt to her feet.

This time, Abrog allowed his cowered opponent to stand. He watched as Izog lifted her falchion and killing knife from the ground. The big hobgoblin chieftain gathered herself for a charge of roaring, cutting, gouging fury. She needed to salvage her pride. Izog was determined to make an example of Abrog.

A long moment passed.

The chieftain charged. Abrog didn't attempt to sidestep or jump back. Either would be certain death. Instead, he stood his ground. Just before the chieftain ran into him, he thrust with the haft of his axe into Izog's neck. It was an impossible move, but for the time being, Abrog was

DANIEL ROY GREENFELD

uncommonly fast and terribly strong. It didn't kill the chieftain, but her charge was stopped. The chieftain's roar turned into a gargle. Instinct prevented her from dropping her weapons, but it wasn't enough to protect her from Abrog's follow-up attack.

Abrog wasted no time. The chieftain died quickly under an avalanche of his blows. Abrog hacked her apart, cleaving through her armor and bone as if it weren't there. She fell to the ground in pieces.

"Abrog is chieftain!" he roared at the tribe. They roared back. Hobgoblins came forward to howl with him, as was tradition with new chieftains. He swept his axe in a circle, keeping them back.

"No!" he shouted at the top of his lungs.

"Under Abrog, things shall be different. No more celebrating while we hide in worthless caves in the dead forest. You hobgoblins have lorded over this tribe eating goblins, yearlings, gobs, and hobs. Then you wonder why there are no more goblin armies. Today things will change!

"No more eating of our own kind. No more killing of our own kind. If we get hungry, we will hunt further. If there is no prey, then we will eat moss and leaves and dirt. From now on, our numbers grow.

"There is an exception. I am exempt from these rules. If anyone disobeys me, if anyone breaks my rules, then I will kill them. They will be consumed by our children, the gobs and hobs. From now on, our numbers grow."

Snarling, one of the hobgoblins asked, "How will we keep the goblins in their place?"

"Their place as breakfast, lunch, and dinner?" said Abrog, mocking the hobgoblin. He projected his voice across the cave and declared, "The goblins will follow my commands. The hobgoblins will follow my commands. All will follow what I command. You are my tribe, and I am life and death. If you disagree, then challenge me singly or altogether. I will kill anyone who disputes me."

Two of the hobgoblins looked at each other and charged. Still energized by eating the cake not so long ago, Abrog marveled at how slow they moved. He chopped his axe into the face of one hobgoblin and blocked the cut of the other with his shield. The impact of the hobgoblin's mace felt light, as if swung by a little gob. Before the second hobgoblin could pull her weapon back for another cut, Abrog buried his axe in her ribs.

As the hobgoblins finished collapsing to the ground, Abrog glared at the tribe. "Anyone else?" he challenged. "Hobgoblins are such easy sport."

Cowed by his speed, brutality, and confidence, the tribe was silent.

"Good. Now we begin. There is much I want to do. Gorgol!" He yelled, naming the goblin hunter who had taken his poor sister Orbag for the pot. He put his axe in his belt.

The hunter slinked up to him nervously, ready to flee. Gorgol didn't need his keen hunter's senses to feel the power and fury that was this young chieftain. As he got close, Abrog stepped forward and lashed out with his fist, knocking the hunter to the ground.

"That was for Orbag." Abrog put his foot on Gorgol's chest, keeping him down. "From now on, you do not hunt our own for the hobgoblins. If you do, you will go in the pot. If a hobgoblin insists, tell me and it's the pot for her. From now it's going to be forest animals for the tribe or nothing."

The new chieftain lifted his foot and pointed at the three hobgoblin corpses. "The tribe will celebrate my rise with a feast. Everyone gets a share!"

As the tribe roared their approval, the cook and his helpers went to work.

Abrog walked over to the dirty furs and swept them off the throne. He sat down and watched the feast. Long into the night, drums were beaten and goblins and hobgoblins stamped their feet. They ate and drank their fill.

Sated by the last of his cakes, he didn't partake in the stew. Even if he was hungry, the thought of eating the dead of his tribe was unappetizing.

Abrog wondered what he had become.

CHAPTER 11

ANNATHEA

The mare wanted to go to another caravan's hay wagons. Annathea wouldn't have any of it. A skilled rider, she used subtle prompts with just the stirrups to guide the horse past the tasty snack. She had always been good with horses, better than any of her brothers. If there was one trait she was happy that she inherited from her mother, it was a love for the big, four-legged animals.

Annathea wore a wide-brimmed brown hat. From her father she had inherited skin that wasn't quite dusky. It still reddened and burned when she didn't cover up. Like her mother, she had long, light brown hair neatly braided into a single cord down her back.

Also like her mother, she was plain, with a face that she felt was too boyish. She thought her nose was a little too flat, her chin perhaps a little too weak. In the past few months her bosom had begun to fill out, yet not yet to the extent that she wanted.

Having grown up riding horses, her posture was ramrod straight, her build athletic. Her black riding dress with long sleeves did nothing to hide her too-broad shoulders. Of course, nothing could hide that she was an inch or so taller than most men.

Hitched to her saddle was the sword that was her birthright as a noble lady. The scabbard was made of fine wood, inlaid with painted, carved tree branches with flowers. Practicing with her blade, as well as the spear, and the bow had given her the wiry arms that just didn't match current fashion. For a noble-trader, practice at arms was a requirement for both safety and leadership.

"Well?" called Sir Oliver, trotting his own horse up next to hers. He matched her pace. His light-skinned round face grinned at her. This was a grin that he didn't share with underlings. He was stocky, of average height, and middle-aged. He had the thick wrists of a swordsman and the posture of a rider. Sir Oliver was her father's cousin. Of the same age as her parents, he was her family's chief retainer, very much an uncle to Annathea.

"All the wagons, horses, and crews appear to be in good shape. Everyone is in their designated place," Annathea said loudly enough for the retainers to hear. Then she said more quietly, "No one questioned my commands today."

DANIEL ROY GREENFELD

Sir Oliver nodded. "That's the way of it, especially for young ladies," he said. "It takes time for the men and especially their wives to not think of you as the little moppet."

"I admit that if I just say things loud enough to be heard, my orders are followed," Annathea admitted with a sheepish smile.

"Annathea, when you were younger we couldn't get you to be quiet. Now we have trouble making you speak up." He grinned.

"How am I supposed to make the crews listen to my orders if you belittle me?" Annathea said, a bit crossly. "I admit one thing and you jump on me for it."

Sir Oliver turned in his saddle and gave a little bow. "Apologies, milady. I meant no disrespect," he said.

Annathea humphed and didn't say anything for a few minutes as they rode the camp perimeter. Even when she demonstrated that she wasn't just a child, but a fifteen-year-old lady, they treated her as if she was a playing child. This was stupid, because she knew not just all the boring, old useless arts of ladyship but also the skills of a modern noble-trader. And she was getting married next year.

"Do you think he remembers me?" she asked Sir Oliver as they finished the last perimeter check and headed inward to her family's pavilion.

"Kuja of the Blue Branches?" he asked. She nodded, confirming that she had changed subjects.

"Annathea, you saw him just last year. That wasn't too long ago. He might remember a child who wasn't interested in him, but you've…ah…grown a little."

"I don't know why I didn't care to talk to him last year. He's to be my husband, yet I spent all my time with the horses and the races."

Sir Oliver clucked his tongue as they arrived at the family pavilion. It was erected on one of the many permanent wooden platforms placed just outside the great walls for this purpose. It was a place for noble-traders visiting the City-State of the Invulnerable Overlord to have a dry camping spot to host and receive guests. He dismounted and handed the reins of his mount to a servant, as did Annathea. Together they walked up the short steps.

As they entered the antechamber of the pavilion, Annathea's mother Samantha came out of the dressing room, garbed in the formal gown of a court lady. She was still taller than her daughter, with none of the baby fat that Annathea couldn't wait to melt away. On the other hand, even with hats and scarves, the rough life of being a noble-trader had put early lines on her face. She

DANIEL ROY GREENFELD

was attended by her lady-in-waiting, Harrieta, Sir Oliver's wife, who was putting the last ribbon in her liege's hair.

"Are things in order?" Annathea's mother asked.

Not even a "please," Annathea thought. This annoyed Annathea as it made the duties her parents assigned her that much more challenging. This was just like how Sir Oliver treated her, except that her mother could, with a single look, dismiss her efforts as completely worthless.

"Yes, mother, they are in order," Annathea confirmed.

Her mother looked past Annathea. She raised an eyebrow at Sir Oliver.

"Yes, milady, your daughter has done a fine job. All the wagons in the right place, and the foremen are performing the pre-market inventory," he replied.

"Then you are finished, Annathea. Get dressed for dinner. Lady Harrieta will attend you." Her mother commanded in that easy way that both annoyed and impressed Annathea.

Dutifully, but excited by the prospect of looking pretty for her betrothed, Annathea walked into the pavilion's "dressing room." Lady Harrieta followed. As they did so, they heard Annathea's mother through the cloth walls of the pavilion. Annathea's mother spoke to Sir Oliver as they walked away.

"Instead of those damned court shoes, I'm wearing my riding boots. Let's check a couple of the wagons to ensure that Annathea didn't mess things up," Samantha said.

Annathea drew in a shuddering breath. Why did her mother treat everything she did as completely untested? It made her so angry. It made her want the wedding tomorrow instead of next year. If only she could move in with her husband's family and never have to listen to her mother's constant barrage of criticism again.

"Don't fret too much, dearie," Harrieta said, motioning to Annathea's formal gown draped across a chair. "It's the way of things. We can never cease thinking about our children as babies."

Annathea nodded but didn't say anything else. Harrieta had helped raise her. As much as Harrieta's husband Oliver was an uncle, Harrieta was an aunt. However, anything Annathea did or said would go into one of Harrieta's ears and come out her mouth as something said to her mother. She had learned that the painful way.

"Do you think he remembers me?" Annathea said, intentionally changing the subject as she unbuckled her sword and pistol belt, hanging it from the chair.

"Absolutely not," Harrieta said. "Last time you were a child uninterested in boys. Now you've become a woman." Harrieta helped her out of her riding dress.

"Harrieta, I'm fifteen to his eighteen. By anyone's accounting that makes me a child to him."

Harrieta turned her around, looked her in the eyes and said, "If you were a child, your parents would not have asked me to be your chaperone tonight."

"What? Why are you my chaperone?" Annathea demanded.

"Because your parents see the same changes I see," Harrieta explained patiently. She picked up the pastel blue formal gown. "They also see how you look at the horse grooms."

"I don't *need* a chaperone. I'm fifteen," Annathea declared.

"Don't be silly," Harrieta reprimanded. "Young ladies aren't allowed unchaperoned. It would soil your family to not have one. You *know* this."

"Does it have to be you? At the fair last month, Dandelion accompanied me."

Harrieta sighed as she helped Annathea into the formal gown. "I know. And it was unseemly. If Dandelion's older brother hadn't been there, thanks to the express warning by my husband, who knows what trouble might have been stirred up?"

"Look, Harrieta, I love you, but this isn't what I want. Ouch!" Annathea cried as Harrieta used a pin to hold the gown in place before fastening the back ties.

"You aren't getting what you want," Harrieta said. "Not today, and not for the rest of your life. You have duties to your family and your retainers. Get used to it, like your elders have done."

"It's not fair. My mother doesn't trust me with anything about the caravan and certainly not with my fiancé," Annathea said. She sulked.

"You should be grateful," admonished Harrieta as she began rebraiding Annathea's long brown hair. "Your husband is only a few years older. He's fit, smart, and handsome. You might even like him. Your parents had a lot of other options, some of them better, but your parents are romantics. They're doing everything they can to make this a love match."

"A love match? Hmm," Annathea mused. "Do you think he'll like me?"

"Let's take a look at my handiwork," Harrieta said. She turned Annathea around in a circle, admiring the results.

Annathea's formal gown was pastel blue, with sleeves that draped cloth like wings, with a very high neck for modesty. Yet the garment was plaited in the right places to display her young, still-boyish figure. This wasn't the current fashion, but it was the right mix of modesty and appeal to meet her aunt and mother's requirements. Instead of a wide-brimmed hat, her head was capped with a wreath of flowers, over which a thin veil of fine cloth was draped. The only thing she would wear from before were her riding boots, for court shoes were not designed with horses in mind.

"I'm pretty certain he'll like you. Right now any young man would like you," the older woman said.

CHAPTER 12

ENGAGEMENT

"Sweet noble heart, I am forbidden to ever see again your fair sweet face which put on the path of love…"

Annathea quietly hummed the minstrel's words to herself as she rode her horse alongside those of her father, mother, Sir Oliver, and Harrieta. Until recently, the songs of minstrels had seemed shallow and meaningless, but now the words carried so much weight.

In just a little while, she would see Kuja again. It was funny how she had protested so much about the marriage for most of her life. Yet now she looked forward to the eternal love that they would share. He would sweep her off her feet, taking her in his strong arms forever.

Her love for him didn't make any sense. In a way it was just like the crush she had had earlier this year on a particular groom. Against her protests, her father had

DANIEL ROY GREENFELD

fired the young man, but now she understood why. She had been a foolish girl, but now she was a woman and Kuja was a man!

Annathea rode her mount sidesaddle. It was the accepted custom when wearing formal court gowns. When she was very little, she had thought it a lovely custom. As she developed her practical riding skills, she had thought it quaint, bordering on stupid. She had argued over practicing it with her mother a hundred times. Now, with the thought of impressing her betrothed, she thanked her mother for being so stubborn. Not that she would tell her mother, because then she would be beset with a hundred "I told you so's."

Their family device recognized by the guards, they passed through the River Gate of the City-State. The massive stone gate and its orichalcum doors made it possible to access the city docks without passing through the City-State itself. Built by the Invulnerable Overlord thousands of years ago in the Third Age, the relief images decorating it had the typically brutalist style of the City-State about them. This gave the gate the same sense of permanence as possessed by the walls and government of the City-State.

Just inside the gate, they passed underneath an elevated railway trestle. Powered by bound elemental spirits, machines called iron dragons would pull wheeled cars around the perimeter of the City-State. The railway connected the different neighborhoods, making travel for commoners and cargo easy. Many of the mountain fasts of the Granite Nation were also linked to this rail system, connecting them and their goods to the river and the world beyond.

Past the River Gate, Annathea and her family were in the dock neighborhood of the City-State. Where the neighborhood was not bordered by the river Krios, the hundred-foot-high walls of the City-State stood guard. The dock neighborhood was where ships and cargo merged their purpose together in trade. A maze of canals took the place of most roads in this neighborhood, allowing the easy movement of heavy goods. At the water's edge, on the sides of roads, even built into bridges, warehouses stood next to inns and craft shops. Every business was dedicated to facilitating trade, or to the selling of goods to people involved in trade. People were industrious here, having little tolerance for slackers or beggars. While crowded, crime-ridden, and smelly, the energy of the docks was overpowering.

On foot, Annathea and her family would have been buffeted and harassed by the darker elements of the dockside crowd. But on horseback they were immune to this, for it was their badge of office as nobility. No commoner would touch a noble, as the Invulnerable Overlord was very generous in its punishment when those of a lower class caused trouble. The very stones of the road and the sides of the canals would tell the Invulnerable Overlord who had been the perpetrator. Justice would be executed against the criminal and their entire family.

DANIEL ROY GREENFELD

Nevertheless, the crowds slowed them down. Hundreds of people conducted their business on the streets, and for them to get out of the way simply took time. Rivermen, merchants, stevedores, craftsmen, and government officials all made way for Annathea's family. Such was the virtue of their right to ride mounts.

To Annathea, nothing about the City-State or class rights mattered. What was important to her was the gigantic blue-painted riverboat, which was their destination. That was the home and treasure of the Blue Branch family, and after next years' wedding, it would be her home as well.

The giant blue boat was shallow-bottomed, intended to ply the Great River rather than any sea. It was strongly built of wood and iron, designed to be well suited for defense. Like Annathea's noble trader family, the Blue Branch's fortune was in cargo, not the pittance of land an ancestor had wrested away from the Stones.

"Why are they flying the black flag?" Annathea's father, Hugh, wondered as they approached.

While an excellent rider, Hugh almost looked comical, as his long legs seemed to be nearly touching the ground. His family were traditionally quite tall, hence their family name "Long Reach."

"Kuja's great-grandmother, Old Lady Blue Branch, has seen ninety summers," said Annathea's mother, Samantha. "I fear the worst."

"I heard that she was a beauty in her youth," commented Harrieta. As Annathea's chaperone, she rounded out their group to an even four.

If Old Lady Blue Branch has indeed passed away, Kuja and his family will be in mourning, Annathea thought. *Kuja will be sad and distraught. I can provide comfort and succor in his time of need! I will be the dutiful daughter to his parents, the comforting sister to Kuja's siblings.*

Annathea's father, Hugh, led his small family onto the docks and to the mooring. They asked for permission to board. It was granted. Leaving their horses behind, they walked up the gangplank. There, they were met by one of the Blue Branch family's senior retainers.

"Hail, Hugh of Long Reach," the retainer said. "I apologize on behalf of my lord. So stricken is he with grief that he will not move."

It was a slight for the Lord of Blue Branch not to greet Annathea's father. However, the circumstances were excusable. "Most understandable," her father reassured the retainer. "If our positions were reversed, I'm certain Lord Kojan would understand as well." Lord Kojan was Kuja's father, grandson of Old Lady Blue Branch.

The retainer nodded. He motioned Annathea's family past a door. There, another retainer met them and led them through hallways and stairs upwards. The stairs ended in a room with couches and six doors, two on three of the walls. Between each pair of doors were small illustrated portraits of family members. One of them had a black cloth draped over it. This was the center of the family bedrooms.

The couches were empty, except for a small boy and a woman. The boy looked five years old, comforted by the woman who had to be his nursemaid. They were both crying.

Annathea, certain it was Kuja's younger brother Durian, rushed forward and knelt by the boy. "Poor thing," she said.

The retainer knocked on a door and entered. He kept the door half open, but Annathea ignored the whispers. She focused on taking care of the boy, who would within a year be her brother-in-law. The retainer came back out, followed by a grim-faced Lord Blue Branch.

Annathea looked up and felt such compassion for him. *Losing one's mother must not be easy*, she thought. Certainly Annathea argued with her mother frequently, but she would be destroyed if her mother were not there.

"You have heard the news, Hugh? What shall we do?" Kojan said, looking Annathea's father in the eyes.

"These things happen, Lord Blue Branch. I'm sure you will persevere. It will be hard, but the unity of our families is something she would have wanted," Hugh Long Reach replied.

"She? Hugh, what do you mean by 'she'?" asked the tearful Kojan.

"Your mother, of course," replied Hugh, uncertainty growing in his voice. "She is aged and at the end of her span of years."

Lord Branch sat in a chair, placed his face in his hands for a minute. Then he looked up at Hugh and said with infinite sadness, "My mother is timeless, as timeless as a golem. It is my Kuja, my eldest son, who apparently is not."

Annathea jumped up so fast that the little boy cried out, and she echoed his cry with her own. "What happened to Kuja?" she asked Lord Branch.

"He...he...." His head slumped. Samantha came over and took his hand. His face in his other hand, he said in a voice full of tears, "It was a stupid accident during cargo loading. A rope snapped. He...he was in the wrong place."

Annathea clapped her hands to her mouth. She felt shock. She felt distant. She felt the recent surge of attraction to the ideal of Kuja fade away in a rush. She had come to grips with the arranged marriage, as did her heart. Now he was gone and, to her disgust, she could barely care.

As Annathea explored her own feelings, she watched as her mother and father comforted Lord Blue Branch. He was a man who would have to bury his own son. She felt for him, but she also worried about herself.

Now that Kuja of the Blue Branches was dead, whom would her parents marry her off to?

Never mind that, she thought. She turned her focus to the crying boy, who was most certainly Durian, Kuja's younger brother.

CHAPTER 13

HOBGOBLINS

The axe flew true this time, the blade sticking into the tree trunk. It wasn't easy to do, for this was not a throwing axe, but a fighting axe. Longer than a hatchet, shorter than a woodcutting axe, the balance and blade were meant for the hack and slash of melee. Yet with a combination of talent and a huge amount of practice, it could serve as a throwing weapon.

Abrog practiced this technique. He knew it gave him an edge in combat. It would be a nice surprise to give an opponent. It was not unlike his unorthodox technique of stabbing with the axe haft, which had contributed to his victory over Izog, the old chieftain. Every trick and useful bit of knowledge would help keep him alive for yet another day.

The hobgoblins were cowed for now, but every chieftain had to deal with challengers. Abrog suspected that he would have more than most chieftains, as the first goblin

DANIEL ROY GREENFELD

ever in the tribe's history to become chieftain. His green skin alone would make him a target.

While the hobgoblins respected strength, to think power was the only thing that motivated them was foolish. They were a conservative lot. During his time as First Goblin, he had discovered that unusual plans gave them pause. They preferred the way things had been done before, be it yesterday or a hundred years ago.

Abrog grunted as he yanked the axe from the tree. To him, this was complete and utter stupidity. The current methods and culture of goblins and hobgoblins were self-destructive. Starving their young, or worse, eating them, meant their numbers would never grow. Goblinkind had become stagnant, hiding in the shadows.

Only the fact that hobgoblins would not consume their own eggs meant that the species survived. Hobgoblins hid their egg clutches in loose, shallow dirt outside the cave, checking on them once a day. If a hobgoblin found their nest opened, the shells broken, the contents eaten, she would become enraged. Any unlucky goblins nearby would be killed.

Hence, goblins left hobgoblin clutches alone, sometimes even protecting them. Even this wasn't ideal, for young that hatched in winter months would immediately be harvested by goblin hunters, ending their short lives in the cooking pot.

Abrog often wondered how he had managed to survive infancy.

He had stopped these idiotic practices as soon as he became chieftain. No more children in the cooking pot or on campfires. No longer did he smell the stench of stewed or roasted goblin flesh.

He yawned. Dawn would be coming soon. It was time to go back to the cave. Yet he lingered for a few minutes. Unlike most goblins, he enjoyed seeing the morning light and could see quite well during the day. It was yet another thing that marked him as being different from his own kind.

He watched the sky lighten, turning golden under the gaze of the sun. The massive, fiery orb was the chariot of the king of gods who hated his kind. It was said that this loathing stemmed from the goblin kings having once conquered the world. The gods wanted their own favorite races to rule instead. They had sent heroes to kill the goblin kings. Chief amongst them was the one who had forged goblin's bane, whose very touch burned goblin skin, flesh, and bone to ash.

Yawning yet again, Abrog decided it was time to go to the cave and rest.

It was not far, but he was exposed to naked sunlight before he got inside. The warmth of the sun was strange and different. Unlike the soothing light of the moon, the sun would eventually heat and burn his skin. Those

DANIEL ROY GREENFELD

who suffered this fate sometimes grew feverish, even dying of sunburn. Therefore, any goblin out in the daylight stayed to the shadows, wore a hood, or slept under thick blankets. The still feral gobs and hobs who remained outside would find crevices and holes to sleep in.

Just inside the cave entrance, the two goblin guards were chewing on bitterroot. It wasn't pleasant, but it would keep them awake for hours. Inside the cave was the dank, dark familiarity of home. Abrog passed from the rough, natural exterior tunnel into the smooth, mined, interior passages. At some point in the tribe's distant past, they had tunneled into the hillside, but the tools and techniques of those days were long forgotten.

He approached his personal chamber, the only one of its kind. As chieftain, it was his right to claim his own interior space. Yet as he did so, he smelled something.

Hobgoblin musk.

He paused for a moment. He felt arousal. Then he felt fear. As First Goblin, he had been selected as a mate by hobgoblins a number of times. It was an unpleasant, violent experience. While he wouldn't be killed during the process (First Goblins having the protection of the chieftain), he had suffered many bruises and nasty bites. Since he had become chieftain, his torment of being selected as a mate had stopped. He had cowed the hobgoblins into submission.

Yet now a hobgoblin in full heat was in his sleeping chamber. A current of fear ran through his heart. He paused.

Then he growled.
I am chieftain! I must show no fear. No matter how I feel, I must respond with strength, he thought.

He stormed into his sleeping chamber. The waiting hobgoblin reached for him, hands open for an embrace. Instead of running or returning the embrace, he rushed forward. He shoved her hard against the stone wall. Her skull cracked against the rock.

"You dare!" Abrog shouted, throwing the stunned hobgoblin to the floor. He recognized her as Lug, strong yet crafty. Readying himself for a fight, he pulled his fighting axe from the hook on his belt.

"I dare," the hobgoblin said from the floor. "I want to mate with the strongest goblin."

"You will not have me," Abrog said. He growled. "Now get out before I split your skull."

Lug stood up, feeling the back of her head. She smiled, displaying her decaying rows of teeth.

"You have already split the skin there. You are the strongest goblin," she said.

The axe trembled in his hand. Her musk was overpowering, and she knew it. Every instinct told him to embrace her, to quicken her eggs. How many times had he seen goblins escape a desirous hobgoblin, only to return to near-certain doom because of the mating instinct?

He had to resist. Everything about this screamed hobgoblin dominance. If he surrendered to his desires, it would mean trouble. His subjects would see this as weakness. The challenges would begin. She was crafty enough to have figured this out and was making a play for the role of chieftain.

Lug slowly moved closer, very aware of the effect she had on him. He knew he had to act before it was too late.

With the speed that was his hallmark as a warrior, Abrog drew the axe back and swung. Her eyes widened, but before she could act, the haft of his axe connected with her temple. The hobgoblin collapsed.

Abrog quickly dragged her out of his sleeping chamber, calling for the cave entrance guards. When they came, he pointed at Lug's unconscious figure and said, "Drag her into the sunlight. If I can beat her off, she can survive the sun's light."

Exhausted from a long day and the effort required to fight off Lug, Abrog returned to his chamber. He collapsed into his sleeping furs.

CHAPTER 14

JUDGMENT

Many of the great buildings of the City-State of the Invulnerable Overlord were tall, lofty constructions rising hundreds of feet into the air. They were the pinnacle efforts of master builders of previous ages.

The architecture displayed an absolute mastery of stone and iron, with graceful bridges, turrets, domes, and towers. They were ornamented with sculpture depicting characters and events from history. These included events, heroes, and gods from the dawn of history to recent ages. Where there was no sculpture, poetry and religious prayer were carved in elegant gilded letters taller than a man.

The Court of Justice did not follow this trend. Instead it was squat and blocky, almost a cube. Instead of decoration by ornaments, the building was engraved with the laws of the Granite Nation. Dispensed over the ages by the Overlord itself, the building was a book

DANIEL ROY GREENFELD

made into stone for any and all to read. That is, should they have the ability to read old golem, of course.

Three months after the day her betrothed passed away, Annathea sat on a hard stone bench in the antechamber of the Court of Justice. It made the calves of her legs hurt to sit on it, but she did not shift her position. It would not do for a bailiff to see her slouching or using the bench as a cot. She had to demonstrate adulthood and maturity if her parents were going to win her case.

She wore a gown purchased for the occasion. It was fashionable for the season—yellow in color, too long for riding or even much walking. It exposed her unfashionably strong-looking arms, yet it was modest otherwise. Her aunt Harrieta had fretted over this. But Annathea didn't care. It wasn't as if the golems could be attracted to mortal flesh. They were made of stone, and created by stone.

Annathea's long brown hair was down, spilling down her back or annoyingly across her face if she leaned forward. As Harrieta said, one did not wear riding braids in the Court of Justice.

Inside the court, where due to her age she was not allowed, the Invulnerable Overlord was determining her case. Actually, it was her fate. While she sat here, the course of her life was being determined by an inhuman immortal from the Third Age.

The golem bailiff keeping watch on the antechamber wandered off, its heavy feet thudding into the marble floor with each step. Like all of its kind, it stood nearly six feet tall. It had a blocky head, broad shoulders, a barrel-like torso, and thick arms.

It had been crafted by its parent by carving stone into the likeness of a golem, animated by a chthonic spirit, and awoken through a mysterious ritual. Now it was immortal. Once animated, the stone became like flesh, malleable and able to bleed, able to heal. Immortal and everlasting, only grievous injury would separate its spirit from its body.

The golem bailiff was one of the true citizens of the Granite Nation, possessing greater rights than any man or women in the land. Such was the way of things.

As soon as the golem bailiff was away, Annathea turned and whispered at Sir Oliver. "How well do you think my father fares?" she said.

"No differently than the last time you asked me this question, Annathea," Sir Oliver whispered back. He wore light armor over which a green surcoat bearing the Long Reach coat of arms had been placed. He seemed uncomfortable without the sword that was normally always at his side.

Annathea sighed. For the hundredth time, she contemplated getting up and pacing. She was certain that Sir Oliver, with his older muscles stiffening, was contemplating the same thing. A cold stone bench, while fine for a golem, could be torture for mortal men.

The great door opened with a booming crack. The noise was startlingly loud. A different golem bailiff emerged. It said with its inhumanly deep voice, "Its Honor has passed judgment. Enter the courtroom and hear the wisdom of the eternal."

Sir Oliver offered his hand and Annathea took it. She thought it silly—she could get up on her own. However, golems demanded propriety, and not following it could hurt her case, even get her family in trouble. Her hand on Sir Oliver's arm, she walked into the courtroom.

The courtroom itself was carved from a single block of perfect stone. Great windows sealed with glass kept the elements outside. At the head of the courtroom sat the immense presence of the Invulnerable Overlord. It sat behind a huge desk on a huge platform, wearing a long, white tunic.

Towering at an amazing ten feet, the Invulnerable Overlord was crafted from a grey vein of granite by one of the smith gods. This occurred in the Third Age, when the secret of chthonic spirit binding had not yet been given to its golem people. Since then it had fought great battles side-to-side with gods. The Invulnerable Overlord gave life to hundreds of golems in the asexual method of its kind. It also founded this city, the greatest the world had ever known. Annathea stared up at it, the Invulnerable Overlord, into its blue gemstone eyes.

Today, the Invulnerable Overlord ruled in its position as Judge. It had listened to the dispute between the two human vassals and was about to pass judgment.

Annathea looked at her parents on one side of the courtroom. Her father nodded at her, hope in his eyes. Her mother kept her eyes on the Invulnerable Overlord. Her mother really annoyed her, but today she was grateful for her mother's irascible nature. If Annathea was going to have anyone fight this argument, it was her mother.

Annathea turned to the parents of her late fiancé, the Blue Branch family. Just months ago her parents were comforting the couple on the other side. Now, they fought in court.

The Invulnerable Overlord's voice was a quiet rumble, like rocks sliding down a hill. "I have weighed the testimony of both sides of this dispute," it said. "I have read the twenty year-old contract between the families. The Blue Branch family wishes for the Long Reach family to honor their contract; that they provide Annathea Long Reach to an eligible heir of Kojan Blue Branch. The Long Reach family states that the contract does not specify a contingency of death upon death of *the heir*; that the contract binding Annathea Long Reach to marriage was broken when *the heir* died."

The Invulnerable Overlord paused for a moment. Then it said, "Complicating this matter is that Annathea Long

Reach is fifteen years old and Durian Blue Branch is five. They would have to wait eleven years for Durian to reach the age of majority before they could be wed."

The Invulnerable Overlord slammed its rocky fist onto the massive stone desk with the weight of an avalanche. "The Granite Nation, like all Golem Nations, is an honorable nation," it said. "We obey to the letter of all contracts and promises. Unless time is specified in a contract, time is not a consideration. My judgment is that in accordance with the laws of the Golem Nations, Annathea Long Reach will marry Durian Blue Branch in eleven years."

Annathea's heart sank. Tears began to flow down her cheeks. A sob escaped her lips.

She and her family bowed in obeisance to the Invulnerable Overlord. Then the bailiffs ushered them out of the room and into the antechamber. There, her father came over and took her in her arms. Meanwhile, her mother shouted at the Blue Branches. "You've made my daughter a spinster!" she said.

"If you had married her to someone else, you would have made my son a cuckold!" Kojan Blue Branch yelled back. "A contract is a contract!"

"Alright then," Hugh Long Reach snarled, still holding Annathea. "We'll honor the contract just like you have. The day Durian turns sixteen is the day that they'll be wed. You won't see her until then, nor will you see an ounce of Long Reach cargo or coin."

"I guess that's how it's going to be," said Kojan Blue Branch, his eyes and voice cold. "We'll see each other in eleven years."

Taking his wife in one arm, Kojan and his family walked out of the antechamber.

Hugh reached a hand to Samantha, his wife and Annathea's mother, inviting her to join their embrace.

Samantha ignored him, stomping out of the Court of Justice. Hugh took Annathea by the hand and followed. Sir Oliver quickly came too, pausing briefly to gather Hugh's and his own sword from the guardsman at the door. Hugh and Annathea followed her mother as she stormed down the steps and across the street into a shop.

Annathea wondered why her mother would go into a stationery store. She might not have gone in if not for her father pulling her in.

"What now?" demanded Samantha angrily once Hugh and Samantha were inside and the door closed. "Are we going to imprison our daughter in a tower for the next eleven years?"

The elderly shopkeeper and her assistant had started to approach, but then they paused when they realized that the noble woman visiting their shop was clearly furious. They backed into the rear of the shop as Sir Oliver entered with two scabbarded swords in hand.

Hugh sighed. "Samantha, two of our sons are wed, running their own caravans," he said.

"What's that supposed to mean?" Samantha demanded.

"It means I'm being realistic," Hugh said. "We'll have heirs soon enough, if not already. And it means that Annathea has other caravans she can join in the next eleven years."

"She'll stay with us," Samantha said firmly.

"No," Annathea said. She felt desperate rage boil up from somewhere inside.

"No?" asked Samantha. "What do you mean by 'no'?"

"I mean no, mother. I'm not going to stay by your side for the next eleven years."

"That's unacceptable. A lady must always be chaperoned."

"Then assign chaperones!" Annathea shouted. "But I'm not going to stay with the caravan like a spinster daughter. This isn't the ancient histories where unwed women waited forever for their true love. It's modern day. I get to have some say in what's going to happen to me."

For a long minute her mother glared at her, fury in her eyes. Annathea glared back. This time she didn't shrink. She was ready to leave, with or without mother and father's permission. She was willing to fight this one out until the very bitter end. If it meant running away, then she was ready to go. She promised herself she would die before she stayed much longer.

Her mother snarled, opening her mouth to scream a reprimand.

Then she snapped her mouth shut.

She opened it again, this time to laugh.

And laugh.

Samantha laughed so hard that tears rolled down her cheeks. This shocked Annathea. It shocked her father too. After this outburst, she had expected the greatest argument of all time with her mother.

Finally, chuckling, Samantha explained, "I'm hard on you, Annathea. As hard as my mother was on me. It wasn't until I got married that your grandma told me that I had impressed her for years. Since you're not getting married for a long time, I'll admit that you've impressed me for a while now. We've all been impressed. These days, you pretty much run the caravan. We just sit back and throw problems your way to force you to adapt and learn."

"What?" Annathea said, jaw dropping.

"You're right, this isn't the histories. Even if we wanted to imprison you in a tower, we can't afford it. Our wealth is in ongoing trade, not the useless scrap of land from which we get our landed status. You, my daughter, are perfectly capable of running the estate."

"Where are you going with this?" asked Hugh.

"I'm not going anywhere," said Samantha. She laughed. "It's Annathea who is going. In a year or three, when she's ready, we'll split the caravan like we did for our sons. She'll take her portion."

Annathea was speechless.

"You won't do it alone," Samantha continued. "Oliver and Harrieta will be your retainers, your chaperones. Your virtue has to remain intact. If worst comes to worst and they pass away, you must find us and stay with us."

Finding her voice, Annathea said, "Why didn't you ever compliment me?"

"I'm not your nursemaid, girl," snapped Samantha. "I'm your mother. My standards are much higher."

Her mother was ready for an argument, so Annathea nodded acquiescently. She didn't want to ruin the deal her mother was offering.

It wasn't marriage…

It was better.

CHAPTER 15

LEVY

The morning sun shone with the luminance of the full moon. Wren walked in a field of black and white flowers, brittle flowers that crunched like bones with each step. He refused to look down. If he did, he knew that he would see something awful.

A tiny voice said his name. He didn't need to look to know that it was the face on one of the flowers. It was his sister Protea's face. Then all the other flowers began calling his name, one of them in Ram's voice. He started running, trying to get away. As he trampled them, the flowers screamed in agony.

There was a hole in front of him. With his running speed pushing him forward, he couldn't stop. He fell into the hole. It wasn't a long drop. He landed in a pile of bones. It was a grave. He struggled to his feet, but the bones clutched at him. He rolled over and looked up.

Standing at the edge of the grave was a dark, cloaked figure looking down at him. The cowl of the cloak was dark, but he knew that inside was himself.

That scared him more than the bones.

Wren's eyes snapped open. It was hard to see, but he knew he was near the hearth of the cabin with his family. It was just another of his nightmares. He trembled in the pre-dawn moments before his family stirred, waiting for the foul dream to dissipate from his memory.

Wren heard his father, Bull, roll off the warm hearth shelf to land on his feet. Unlike Wren and more like Ram, their father was burly and strong. With grey hair revealing that he was no longer a young man, their father still won the yearly strength contests played on midsummer's day. Now on his feet, Bull said loudly enough to wake the whole family, "Time to get to work."

Wren carefully made his way out of the loft, tagging along with Ram and Protea. Even though their older sister had married and moved into her own home in the village, the loft no longer felt roomy. They were older and bigger now, especially the sixteen-year-old Ram.

Ram was taking after his father. He was tall and thewed like a wrestler, possessing seemingly unending reserves of strength and endurance. He was even wearing an old tunic and trousers that were once worn by Bull. He had dark brown hair that matched Wren's own, framing a face that was often grinning. While mighty in strength, he relied on Wren's intelligence.

Besides the hair, Wren looked very different. He was scrawny and got tired easily. When they were younger his mother had babied him, but for the past year she had begun to expect more of him. The problem was that as willing as Wren was to do work, he was still too small and frail to do much. He liked to think that he made up for this by being more intelligent, but, deep inside, he knew this wasn't true. Unlike Ram, Wren inherited his clothing from the neighbor's ten-year-old son, who was already taller than Wren.

Protea, their little sister, flipped her long, black hair onto her back. Then, quick on her feet as always, she descended first down the ladder. Their mother clucked at her to help at the hearth.

Protea had finally noticed boys last month, just as her body was beginning its transformation from girl to woman. She had been found in the arms of Finch just days ago.

Wren couldn't understand why she liked Finch. Wren thought he was an annoying jerk, always insulting. Since that day, their mother kept Protea under a watchful eye, often complaining that their daughter was the cause of the grey beginning to dominate her otherwise dark hair.

Wren descended the ladder next, with Ram right behind him. He took his cloak from the peg at the door and handed Ram his own. Then they quickly exited, not wanting to spoil the heat of the house with the cold air of early spring. The two brothers walked to the covered woodpile, where Wren stacked piece after piece of cut wood in Ram's strong arms. Ram carried the wood because for his age Wren was terribly small and weak. His parents lived in eternal fear of him getting sick. Under their overprotective watch, he had not had a sniffle for as long as he could remember.

Wren walked back to the door and opened it for his brother. Then he turned to the chicken coops built into the side of the house.

He stopped.

In the village square he saw four dryads on horses and two weald hounds.

He had never seen dryads before, but they fit the description perfectly. Their faces were impossibly beautiful, without a wrinkle or mark. They were clad in wonderfully simple, light garments on a cold, early spring morning, yet they didn't seem to notice the chill. Their clothing was shiny. It seemed to catch the morning sun and illuminate the whole village. The dryads did not bother with caps or helms, letting their long, green or brown hair flow freely. Long, elegantly-pointed ears pushed out from the sides of their heads. Their feet were bare. The three male dryads looked noble and majestic, and the female was all of that, yet she was also so lovely that she made his eyes ache. All the passions of a fifteen-year-old boy flooded his senses.

The lady dryad, as if noticing his attraction, turned to look at him. Her eyes seemed to peer deep into Wren's soul.

Wren darted into the house. Not taking care with the door, it swung wide open. His father ordered, "Hey! Close the damned door!"

"There are dryads in the village!" Wren shouted.

There was a mass bustle to gather cloaks, get outside and greet the honored visitors. Wren and his family might be peasant farmers in service to the knight-magistrate, but even he was just a vassal of the dryad overlords. Dryads provided the land with protection from monsters, wild beasts and the depredations of the Golem Nations. The light of the beacon from their distant Tower of Sorcery brought rain during drought, banished locusts from the fields, and even provided relief from plague.

As the family emerged, they saw the knight-magistrate, his squire, and two retainers join the dryads. Wren could not help but notice that Sir Aethel, who normally seemed extravagant in his arms and armor, looked quite poor next to the magnificence of the dryads. Even the tall, elegant horses that Sir Aethel and his men rode were like mangy nags compared to the mounts of the dryads.

Together, the dryads and the men trotted out of sight, heading towards the village square.

The village temple bell began to toll for assembly in the village square. Forewarned by Wren, his family made it there before the bustle of everyone trying to arrive at once.

Wren's father strategically kept them in the middle of the square. This way they wouldn't be at the front as everyone filed in, nor would they be at the back.

"Why do you think they are here?" Wren's mother asked.

"Perhaps the rumors of war are true," his father responded.

Once the village had assembled, Sir Aethel called for silence. As always, he was only partially effective. Many people just kept talking.

"I am Zelkova, marshal of the levy," one of the lady dryads said. She had a quiet, slightly accented voice that somehow cut through the cold wind of early spring and the voices of the gossiping crowd. The village went completely silent at this simple display of effortless power. It put to shame the attempts of visiting minstrels to portray dryads.

Gasps were heard across the square. Wren's mother put her hand to her mouth, stifling a sob.

The dryad spoke again in her strangely beautiful voice, "We need fifty young men, preferably unmarried and without children. They will serve as levy, journeying with us across the Rainbow Mountains to come to grips with the golem foe. That is enough for this village to maintain its one-in-ten harvest quota and keep everyone fed."

There was an intake of breath across the village. A baby started to cry. A mother started to raise her voice in complaint.

"I've been ordered to lead you," Sir Aethel shouted in his gravelly voice. "My wife stays behind as steward until the day I return from beyond the Rainbow Mountains. If I can make sacrifice in return for the bounties the dryads provide, so can you. All unmarried men older than fourteen years, please step forward."

Wren felt a shock of excitement and fear of disappointment run through him. At age fifteen, he was old enough to march to war! On the other hand, he was so small that they might not take him. He stepped forward and Ram followed.

His mother yanked him back by the hood of his cloak.

"Don't worry, Peony," said his father loudly, pulling his wife's hand free. "They won't take Wren or Ram. One is too small and the other is too stupid."

As Bull pushed Wren forward, Wren heard both his father's words and the snickers of quiet laughter from the neighbors. His head hung low in embarrassment. He would never live this down. Tears began to fall from his eyes. Ram sensed his brother's anguish. He put his arm around him in comfort.

Sir Aethel and the dryads dismounted. The dryads were as tall or taller than any of the human warriors. They walked past the young men standing at the front of the crowd. Knowing the people of the village and many of the boys by name, the knight chose carefully. When a young man was chosen for the levy, he would stand taller. When the young man was skipped over, he shrunk.

As they neared Wren the same heartbreakingly lovely dryad who had seen Wren turned and walked through the crowd to a family who lacked any sons. She knelt by their youngest daughter, a girl of age nine, and put her hand on her head. She whispered something to the wide-eyed girl, who nodded with the seriousness of a child. The dryad stood up and joined her waiting comrades.

Sir Aethel walked past Wren and Ram. His eyes glanced at them, then he walked past them. Wren heard his mother sigh in relief right behind him.

Instead of walking past, the dryads stopped. The lady dryad stepped closer to tower over Wren. Up close, her inhuman nature overcame the beauty that he had seen from afar. On the exposed skin of her face and hands, he could see what looked like a wood grain pattern. Her hair was actually made up of strands of colored vine, which he knew would sprout flowers during the right season. She smelled of pine. He felt a glow of power tingle his face and hands.

"This one has the gift of magic. He will be taken to the Tower of Sorcery," she said.

Wren blinked.

He had the talent! He would have power! He would be a hero! Once trained, no one could mock him for his small stature ever again.

"Me too!" shouted Ram at the top of his lungs.

Everything seemed to stop for a long minute. One did not give orders to dryad overlords. He had seen men whipped by Sir Aethel's retainers for not demonstrating the proper respect to him.

To everyone's relief, the lady dryad smiled. Her teeth were like polished white pine wood. When she spoke, he noticed that the inside of her mouth was the same color as her teeth. Wren had never seen anything so strange, yet so beautiful.

"Such brotherly devotion," she said. "If you serve in the levy, you may accompany him on the journey to the Tower. Inside the Tower, he will be safe. When the army and your brother Wren are trained and begin their marches, you may accompany him as his retainer. Do you agree to this?"

Ram nodded.

"I must hear you," she insisted.

"I agree."

His mother and sister Protea wailed in grief. They took turns hugging Wren and Ram. Then they let them go and ran back into the house to get things for the journey. While they ransacked their home for supplies, their father pulled them close for a moment and told them to take care of each other.

Bull stepped back, tears in his eyes. "When I see you next I expect you to be a mighty warrior and sorcerer," he said.

Their mother and sister came back bearing bedrolls, spare tunics, food for the road, and good luck charms. Soberly, their mother gave Ram the spearhead used by their great-grandfather in the last levy call-up.

Sir Aethel called out. "The dryads have decided that it is now time to go," he said.

The young men followed the dryads and knight out of the square. As they did so, Wren heard Protea call out Finch's name.

Wren looked back. To his disgust, he saw her embrace and kiss Finch. He had grown tall, slim, and handsome. He was now the type of teenage boy who attracted girls. His older brother, Sparrow, laughed and slapped his younger brother on the back. Then their father, Bull, barged in, yanking his daughter from her first love. With his meaty hand, he shoved Finch away.

"Promise me you'll come back!" Protea shouted as their father pulled her away.

"I will!" Finch said. Sparrow prodded him along.

At that moment, Wren decided that he truly hated Finch. When he learned magic, he would curse him into the grave.

The fifty young men were marched away from the square, through the gate, out of the village, and down the road. The villagers followed them to the edge of the furthest field. As the boys marched into the forest, Wren and the others looked back to catch one last glimpse of their families.

The dryads rode in the front, accompanied by Sir Aethel and squire. In an hour, Wren commented to Ram that they were further than most of them had ever been in their lives. Ram nodded. As always, he didn't say much. Many of the other young men were excited to be on this journey.

The woods they marched through cleared at midday as they reached the neighboring village of Grunswald. They were instructed to wait as the dryads and Sir Aethel fetched another lot of young men for the levy. Once this lot was down, they were all marched into the woods until it was dark and the men stumbling. Wren's feet and legs ached.

There was no rain that night, but it being early spring, it was rather cold. The men lit fires with wood that they scavenged from the floor of the forest—woodcutting being quite illegal in Dryad domains. Everyone huddled together and shared food. Ram and Wren shared food with each other. They sat mostly apart from the other boys from the village.

The dryads kept apart, and Sir Aethel stayed near them. To Wren, the knight seemed proud to sit and break bread with dryads. It was the same look he had seen on his great-grandfather when Sir Aethel had come to pay his respects on his death bed. He supposed that they were all vassals to those immortal creatures, and that knights were just exalted servants.

One day, Wren, swore to himself, he too would be an exalted servant. Or perhaps something even greater.

CHAPTER 16

RAID

Abrog stood alone, away from the goblins and hobgoblins. Earlier in his life, he would have cowered with the other goblins, feeling strength in their proximity. Now, he relished being away from the pushing, pinching, and grunts of his comrades. It gave him more time to think. Thinking was what kept him alive. Killing challengers was one way for a chieftain to survive, but the other way was to never have a failure. A chieftain's failures could cause all kinds of problems, such as murder while sleeping. Chieftains usually had room for some failure, but he had none because he was already boldly breaking the tradition of cannibalism. The hobgoblins, the backbone of the tribe, really didn't like that they no longer had easy meals of their smaller kin.

The irony of it was that Abrog was pretty certain that during the glory time of goblin kind, the cannibal tradition didn't exist. There was no way the Dark Lord could have marshaled the ancient armies while goblin kind consumed their own.

Realizing his thoughts were drifting from the present, Abrog refocused himself.

He could see that, through a short stretch of woods, across a wooden fence, were the fields of a human village. So confident were they of their golem protectors that they didn't even have defensive walls. It infuriated him. There had once been a time when every settlement had defenses to keep his kind at bay.

Abrog stood between the village and his tribe, not yet trusting them to wait until his signal to attack. This was the first attack of the tribe on a human village in many years. He knew that his still undisciplined tribe wouldn't follow any order but to move in quietly and then attack with noise and fury. They would kill and destroy anyone or anything they encountered, unless Abrog directly intervened. He sighed internally, for legend had it in the old days goblins took slaves.

It was now dark. There were no more lanterns in the village to see. Abrog wanted to wait longer, but the tribe was getting restless. It was dangerous for a chieftain to lose control of his tribe in idle moments. Better to encourage them to do what they wanted to do.

He grunted, raising his axe above his head. Then he pointed it at the town, signaling the attack. Quietly, he began moving forward. Behind him, his tribe moved forward, making what seemed to be a hideous amount of noise. He shrugged and kept moving.

The wooden fence was easy to climb. In moments he was on the other side, tramping through young crops. It was his first time in such a thing, and he was tempted to stop and examine them. They certainly smelled better than forest moss and bark.

Now was not the time. The village lay ahead, free for the taking.

As he approached the village, his eyes, much sharper than those of his comrades, picked out the symbol of crossed hammers on the village. His confidence drained away, and he stopped. The hammers meant that this town was under the protection of the golems.

Behind him, his tribe stopped as well. He needed to keep going. If he didn't, he would die in his sleep. He had to demonstrate fearlessness if he was going to succeed and stay alive.

He took a small step, then another, this one bold and strong. He willed himself into a run. Behind him his tribe howled and followed.

Dogs started to bark their warning. The livestock of the humans began to bleat, honk, and gobble in consternation. The soft, sibilant cries of the humans followed. Abrog didn't slow, and he felt the rush of his tribe behind him.

The same hounds that sounded the original alarm came bounding out of the village, racing toward him at a pace no goblin could match. For a moment he worried, because wild dogs sometimes caused problems for goblins. They weren't as large or intelligent as the pony-sized wolves, but he knew that some of the larger, stockier dogs could be incredibly ferocious.

The dogs saw the onrushing mob of goblins and skidded to a halt. It was one thing for a band of dogs to prey on a few goblins, but it was another thing for them to face the hundred howling hobgoblins and goblins that made up a tribe. They turned and bolted, scattering in every direction except towards Abrog and his tribe.

Then Abrog was in the village itself, with his tribe a pace behind. A door opened to his left. A human as tall as Abrog stuck out his bearded head. Abrog slammed his shield into the man, knocking him back into the building. Knowing that his tribe was right behind him, Abrog moved deeper into the village.

The village wasn't very large. In moments he was in the center, standing by a well. He picked one of the closest buildings at random and charged the door, leading again with his shield. Abrog slammed into the door. It did not break as he expected. He winced at the new bruise on his shoulder and backed away for a moment. While the

DANIEL ROY GREENFELD

door looked very stout, the shutters on the windows looked like things that his axe could deal with handily.

He dropped his shield. Then with strong, practiced strokes, he quickly chopped away at the hinges of the shutters. As he did so, the rest of his tribe attacked the buildings and residents of the village, or at least they attempted to get in. Some of the goblins, seeing what he was up to, also began to attack the other windows of this house. One of them had even climbed onto the thatched roof and was trying unsuccessfully to worm his way through.

As soon as Abrog broke the window open, a goblin jumped through it before he could, yelling, "Lemme in!"

Abrog followed in through the window but stopped just as he crossed the windowsill, a bristled pole catching him mid-leap. The holder of the strange pole was bowled over. Abrog saw that the goblin had fallen clumsily on his back just inside. He saw another human swing a woodcutting axe at the downed goblin, who shrieked as it sliced off the goblin's ear.

Putting his free hand on the windowsill, Abrog climbed all the way in. He used his momentum to swing his own axe deep into the human's skull. The human dropped like a stone, wrenching Abrog's axe from his hand.

There were other humans in this house, both large and small. All of them were screaming, gibbering in their weak-sounding, sibilant tongue. One of the smaller ones, clearly a youngling, raced to the fallen human, wailing in grief.

"Right, I'll do you for that!" snarled the goblin who was missing his ear. He stood up and raised his falchion for a cut that would certainly kill the youngling human.

Abrog watched with terrible fascination as the youngling human lived out what was going to be the last few moments of her short life. Like Orbag, she would never again have the chance to play games, make more friends, and serve her chieftain. Abrog felt a wrenching tear in his heart as his grief for Orbag was rekindled.

As the falchion came down, Abrog shoved the earless goblin aside, spoiling the strike. "No!" he shouted.

The earless goblin stumbled and fell. Abrog took this time to turn back to the window, to shove back the other goblins trying to jam their way inside.

"This place is my plunder! These humans are my slaves!" Abrog roared.

"I want vengeance for my ear. If I can't get it from the humans, I'll get it from you," growled the earless goblin as it struggled to rise in the growing mess of the house.

Abrog didn't wait for the treacherous goblin to gain his feet. He leapt onto him barehanded, pinning him to the ground with his superior strength, skill, and weight. His sharp teeth tore out the goblin's throat.

Abrog came back up again, this time holding the now dying goblin's falchion. He ignored the cowering humans, shouting at the goblins gawking from the window. "Find me rope or chain to bind my slaves. Then go and take loot for yourselves," he said.

DANIEL ROY GREENFELD

CHAPTER 17

PRISONERS

An hour passed.

"Here are the chains from the smithy," the goblin said to Abrog, dumping his load on the ground.

"Bind the humans. Do not harm them, or else we'll be eating you for dinner," Abrog said.

"But, but I want to get me some loot," the goblin whined.

Abrog shoved the goblin away, tripping his underling as he did so. The minion sprawled in the dirt, then slowly got to his feet. He complied with his order.

As the goblin did his bidding, the few prisoners taken during the raid trembled in even more fear and shock. Abrog expected some of them to die of fright before the night was over. He didn't intend to kill them; on the contrary, he needed them alive and healthy. Humans had skills that goblinkind lacked. He wanted to use them and learn from them.

A hobgoblin came out of a nearby peasant hut, splashed with blood, drinking from a bottle, grinning with pleasure. She noticed Abrog and his loot. Raising her chopping sword to the night sky, she howled, "Kill them all!"

Ignoring Abrog, the hobgoblin charged at the bound captives, who cringed and cried their fear. Blinded by her lust for destruction, she did not even notice him. Abrog stepped into her path, his fist connecting with her face. The impact shook him. The blow took the hobgoblin off her feet.

She lay stunned on the ground long enough for Abrog to wonder if he had killed her. Then she groaned and tried to make her way to her feet. Still dazed by running into his fist, her legs wobbled. Clearly, finding her balance was a challenge.

Abrog walked up to her. "These are mine!" he yelled into her ear.

The hobgoblin flinched at the blast of noise in her ear. She placed her hand protectively to the side of her skull and backed away.

It is a shame that my goblins killed everyone they have at their mercy, Abrog muttered under his breath. *It had been tragically stupid. Humans would make good slaves.*

The strongest of them could even grow to join the tribe. Losing the children was wrong in a way he felt in his chest. He grieved for them the same way he grieved for Orbag and all the gobs and hobs who hadn't grown up.

Deep in his thoughts, Abrog didn't notice the tears welling up in his eyes.

In the future he would have the children spared.

The village, while marked as being protected by golems, had been ripe for plucking. There had been no defense. Humans had been much easier prey than deer or wild pig. The slaughter was quickly over and the looting begun. When they saw him, the members of his tribe cheered him. Abrog had brought them success beyond their petty dreams.

He watched as his minions struggled to carry their loot away. They carried overflowing bags and chests in their arms. Over their shoulders draped the carcasses of small livestock. One goblin stuck a dozen knives and a hatchet into his belt. Somehow he also managed to carry a bow, two spears, a shovel, a pitchfork, and his own shield in his hands. As he walked past Abrog, the goblin lost his grip on something, and everything clattered to the ground.

"If we had kept the livestock alive, we could have just tied the loot to them and led them away," Abrog said.

The goblin's face went from displaying victorious joy to sad disappointment. He sighed and started to pick up his stolen tools and weapons. Abrog then realized that nitpicking his minions in victory might cause problems later.

"Do not be sad. We won," Abrog said. "Relish in your success and your choice of loot. Goblin smiths are not as good as human smiths."

The goblin's face brightened. "Aye, master. My chopper broke in the fighting," he said.

"That's why you are so eager to take their weapons," Abrog said. "Next time we'll have a band of goblins capture livestock so we can carry more."

He turned to face his prisoners again, now studying them. Some of his prisoners were female. He was surprised that it was trivially easy to tell human genders apart. Indeed humans were very different than goblins.

"The golems will kill you!" said one of the weeping women.

Abrog blinked, then turned in shock. He didn't speak the human tongue, and he couldn't have understood it, could he?

"Golems," Abrog said. He repeated one of the words she had said, the soft syllables hard to form with his fangs getting in the way.

"Yes, the golems. They will come here with hammers and might. They'll kill each and every one of you," she said. The woman spat.

"I understand you," Abrog said with difficulty. In his heart he worried about golems pursuing his band. No one he knew had ever faced them before, but they were old enemies of the goblins. It was said that they were carved from stone, had magical powers, and even invented bang powder.

The woman glared at him through tears.

Perhaps he could turn this prisoner to his advantage, Abrog mused. Humans were supposed to be smarter than goblins, but Abrog was the smartest goblin of them all. He would attempt a trick he used at times to get information out of recalcitrant goblins.

"How could the golems possibly catch us?" he asked. He laughed at his prisoner.

"They will bring dogs. They will scent out your trail and find you," she said.

His trick worked! She had given him what he needed to know!

Abrog filtered out the cries and pleas of the captives. As much as his curiosity and pity made him want to talk to them, he had his tribe to look after.

He had not thought of golems using dogs for tracking, but it made sense. He had seen foxes hunt with their noses, and dogs were said to be cousins of foxes and wolves. Unlike foxes and wolves, dogs were enslaved to the humans as their guardians and helpers. In fact, during the attack on the village, the dogs were the only ones to attempt a defense. He hadn't known that golems used dogs as well, but it made sense if their human slaves used them.

In any case, Abrog and his tribe were now in terrible danger. He ignored the curses and insults of the prisoner. He focused on finding a way to bring his tribe home safely.

He remembered not long ago when two goblin hunters died when they had stumbled into a bear while chasing a deer. Without their skills, there had been a lot less food and the tribe had been hungry for a while until Gorgol trained new hunters. Since then, he recognized that skilled goblin hunters were more useful to the tribe than tough hobgoblins.

If he equated the dogs to the hunters, would killing them allow his tribe to escape?

No one in the tribe had fought golems in living memory, but there were legends. Golems were said to be hard to kill. Their skin was as tough as stone, even if they had flesh underneath the solid outer layer. They wore heavy armor tirelessly and carried crossbows, guns, well-crafted axes and hammers. Killing the dogs in a direct fight with golems present would be hard, so it would have to be done sneakily. Fortunately, he grew up as a sneaky gob and knew how to be cunning and tricky under the right circumstances.

Reports from a few goblins were that at least one human had managed to escape the raid on horseback. This meant that Abrog had a lot to do. The tribe needed to flee into the forest. The hunters needed to get to work on killing those dogs.

DANIEL ROY GREENFELD

CHAPTER 18

TRAP

Hours passed. During this time, Abrog sent most of the goblins and all of the hobgoblins ahead to the cave. He kept the hunters with him. Their skills and bows were what he needed—not axe, falchion, cleaver, or club. They needed to stop the pursuit cold, before it led the enemy right to his tribe's cave.

Gorgol had found them the perfect ambush spot. It was inside a gully with a floor of leaves and a few fallen branches the size of logs. Abrog and the hunters blazed an extremely obvious trail into the gully, going all the way until it opened up again. Then they clambered up and around the steepest slope, which put them in high ground. The advantage of this spot was the pursuers would come around a bend half-blocked by thorny bramble into perfect bow range. If the goblins were charged, accessing them would require climbing up a steep surface that would take two hands to climb.

Indeed, this was the perfect spot for an ambush. Abrog and his underlings now waited for their targets through the dregs of the night and into the next day.

Abrog still felt bitter towards Gorgol. He missed his sister, Orbag. The irony was that he knew that should she have lived. By now they would have been separated anyhow, possibly even forgetting that they were ever siblings. It was only due to the accident of her death that he had found the magical food that had transformed him, allowing him to keep his memories of his ordinarily forgotten youth.

Abrog looked at the goblin hunters to either side. They were nervous, but their hunting craft and his presence kept them still and quiet. In a little while, not far away, dogs barked. Men and golems cursed as they crashed through the brambles. Soon they would find the gully and then run into Abrog and the hunters.

As the first dog pulled its handler into sight following the gully trail intentionally left by the goblins, Abrog readied his bow. It was a hunting bow one of his minions had looted at the village. For a moment he studied the beast and man.

The dog was larger than a fox, and stockier too. Yet it was smaller than a wolf. It was excited by the chase, as if it were a game. Abrog had a sudden realization that dogs thought this way. It occurred to him that, unlike the ravenous, foul-minded wolves that raided the woods during the winter, this creature was as a child. The dog's

DANIEL ROY GREENFELD

world wasn't about chasing down the hated foe, but about winning the game of catching something.

What had been a solid plan in his head now seemed wrong. It all felt like a waste.

It was too late, though. In moments they would be discovered and the ambush spoiled. He had to go through with his plan or risk the prepared wrath of the golems. More dogs and their human handlers came into sight. Behind them, he heard a strange, heavy tread that had to be golems.

Knowing that his ten goblin hunters had already marked their targets, he took aim as well. "Fire!" he commanded.

Abrog and his goblin hunters loosed their arrows down the slope of the gully and into the dogs. No arrow had been aimed at the human handlers, but rather their pets. The hounds yelped in pain. Just as when the human children had been murdered last night, Abrog felt a strange pain in his chest.

The dog handlers unleashed their charges, and the uninjured hounds launched forward like arrows. Abrog quickly pulled his second arrow from the dirt and put it to his bow. He drew the string to his ear and aimed at a hound with spots all over its body. The animal was going so fast that he knew it would be a challenging shot. Before he could shoot, the hound was at the base of the slope. He watched with astonishment as it used its velocity to propel itself upwards a great distance before its momentum ceased. The hound looked him in the eye, barked at him, tried to scramble the rest of the way.

It was almost as if Abrog could understand the dog. The dog knew Abrog was the scent that it was trained to track down. It was very close to winning its game. It might wrestle and bite him, but, unlike a wolf, it wouldn't go for his throat.

Abrog loosed his arrow, taking the dog in the throat. It collapsed, tumbled back down the slope, snapping the arrow with a crack. Mortally injured, it looked him in the eye as its blood spilled from its ragged throat. He felt its pain, its fear. How lonely it was at the bottom of the slope, away from its pack and master. Then something faded and the dog was no more.

Rather than feeling joy at killing his first prey with a bow, Abrog felt pity for it.

He shook it off. It was time to go. Having loosed both arrows into the dogs, the goblin hunters were already melting into the woods. Abrog joined them. Together, they ran as fast as they could as the men behind them hurled insults, while the slower and infinitely more dangerous golems fired arquebuses.

Quickly, the goblin hunters threw off the chase, leaving the humans and golems far behind. Abrog, once he was certain he had lost the foe, made his way to the officially designated meeting place, a clump of rocks large enough to sit on. Over the course of the next two hours and sunset, all the goblin hunters found their way there.

Abrog was delighted. Not only had he organized the first successful raid on a human village since anyone could remember, but he had done it without a single casualty.

However, he felt that odd pain for seeing the children die, and for killing the dog. This feeling was alien to him. And it would not go away. He felt pain at seeing young die—looking into their eyes, watching them go still. Their violent passing made him think about his own youth.

He remembered his own losses at the hands of others. He remembered losing Orbag, but what about the others in his clutch? He couldn't remember them. He didn't know if they lived. Were they all food for the pot, or did they fight alongside him? As close as he had been to his sister, he wondered if the hounds had been just as close to their packmates.

He hated this feeling of causing the same kind of anguish that he had suffered. He wanted it to go away. He didn't want to kill anymore. But he knew that if he stopped killing, his tribe would see it as a weakness and rise up against him.

Now he understood why the other races hated and cursed his kind. All that goblins and hobgoblins did was ruin and destroy with little remorse. They were extremely proficient at it, especially him.

The tragedy of the destructive path was that it was inefficient, self-defeating. Without a strong leader like the Dark Lord of days long gone to control their base natures, goblins ravaged themselves even more than they did others. It was why they hid in the forest, and why they skulked in the shadows.

There had to be a better way.

Abrog thought about his captives, especially the female prisoner that provided very useful information. With that knowledge, he had quite possibly saved his tribe. He had named her and her family as his slaves, his property. Perhaps that was the way?

Old goblin legends didn't just mention the Dark Lord. They mentioned slaves who did as their goblin masters bid. Until now, Abrog had never considered what that meant.

Perhaps the answer was slavery?

He would try it and see. Anything to end the useless slaughter, he thought.

Trap   155

CHAPTER 19

INTO THE BRAMBLES

Wren's feet and legs were stiff. He shuffled forward painfully. Everyone had recovered in the first few days of the march. If not for his brother Ram taking his entire load and even carrying him from time to time, he would have fallen behind.

For the adventure of a lifetime, it was quite an inglorious beginning. He should have known that the reality would be quite different than his imagination. Sometimes he was afraid that the Tower of Sorcery would be yet another disappointment, but then he would remember the confidence of Zelkova, the lady dryad, back in Perswald. She had selected him. She had smiled her strange, not-human smile at him. He took heart and resolved to keep his hopes up.

In the morning of the second day, before the march began anew, Wren and Ram found fallen branches that could serve as walking sticks. Using their knives, they

DANIEL ROY GREENFELD

stripped off the lesser branches and cut away the rough edges around comfortable hand height. In the evening, when then had more time, they smoothed their walking sticks down even more.

Wren, Ram, their fellow villagers, and the rest of the army marched across field, forest, and hill. They headed toward the Rainbow Mountains far, far in the distance. Human villages dotted the land. The small group of young men swelled in numbers as the dryads and a growing force of knights assembled the levy. Wren had never seen so many people in his life. Soon, hundreds of young men formed a long column that wound through the land.

Many of them spoke in funny accents. Some wore funny tunics and trousers. Others had odd names for peasant boys, being named after things that weren't animals. Wren and Ram heard awkward peasant names like "Rock," "Tree," "Harvest," and "Candle" being called out. Fights broke out over these differences or imagined slights. The knights broke these up quickly. Instead, the knights spoke of duty and service. The enemy wasn't each other, but the golems beyond the Tower of Sorcery. The golems were the reason they marched. For the men to fight each other was helping the hated enemy.

The knights would point at the Tower, so tall that on the clearest days it could be seen rising just above the mountains in the distance. This was the heart of their land, their nation. The duty of every man, knight or peasant, was to assist the dryads in protecting their nation.

Ram and Wren stuck closely to the other young men from their region: either their own Perswald or neighboring Grunswald. That meant that in the evenings, they shared their fire with neighbors and cousins. Together, they sang old, familiar songs. But they stayed away from their old playmates Ox, Sparrow, and Finch. Wren had never forgiven them for the indignities of childhood. Even if he had, they weren't so kind to let him forget. He hated their taunts, especially Finch's quick, cruel wit.

Ram stayed by his side constantly. Wren knew it wasn't just brotherly affection. No, Ram was protecting him. His presence kept trouble away, but Wren could sense the laughter around them. He knew he was the butt of jokes, as was Ram. Wren also suspected that Finch was telling lurid stories about his sister behind their backs.

Like many of the other young men, Wren and Ram tried to catch game with their slings. Unfortunately, they had so much competition for hunting that they had little luck at all. Instead, their meals consisted of food provided by the accompanying wagons. Their diet was mostly barley, oatmeal, beans, and nuts, always made into porridge. Men would supplement that with whatever they could find, which was mostly the plentiful wild onions that grew in the meadows that dotted the countryside, and occasionally game. As spring passed and the days lengthened, the men began to find berry patches producing sweet, tart berries. All of them—blackberries, raspberries, blueberries—were highly coveted and hurriedly picked over by men braving thorn and poison ivy.

Over the days and weeks, the road went into wilder lands. In these lands, the dryads did not rule the forest. Other creatures of the wilderness did. No human villages were here to collect more men from. All that lay before them was the never-ending road. The path grew more jagged, winding round and round through craggy hills and dangerous-looking forests. Wolves howled at night, singing to each other the details of their hunts. Bandits and outlaws made the wilderness their home, as did much more terrible things. If they did not consist of an army of at least a thousand, Wren would have been afraid.

Now, their rations were supplemented by magic. Every morning, each man would be instructed to collect a single, fallen acorn from a particular type of oak that no peasant had ever seen before. This strange breed of tree was deemed a "tanoak" by the dryads. The fifteen knights would form a circle around the dryads, and the men formed a crowd that surrounded the knights. The dryads would sing a spell that ended with a green burst of light. That night, the men would heat their acorns in campfires until they popped into loaves of savory, nutty bread. The loaves were delicious and filling, and they left a lingering, warm feeling throughout the body.

Even though it was late spring, the nights were very cold. The men ranged further and further to find acceptable fallen branches and dead trees for their cooking fires. Their direct overlords, the knights who lorded over small groups of villages, guarded them carefully as they ventured off the path. The dryads would sometimes walk into the woods with their weald hounds and disappear for the time. This was to be expected, because the dryads were the eternal forest lords.

Then, one day, the road seemed to vanish into a tunnel of ten-foot-high twisted, blackened bushes covered with thorns six inches long. Each thorn gleamed as if forged of iron. There were frightened whispers that the thorns might be poisoned. Strange bird calls could be heard from within. The squawks and chittering noises coming out of the bushes were painful to the ear, like desperate cries on the edge of madness.

The dryads, male and female, brought the column to a halt in a sizable clearing, without tree or bush, covered by knee-high grass. They waited for everyone to come within hearing distance. This took a long time, for the army had grown to over a thousand men of common birth, fifteen knights, and the four dryads. Once assembled, the leader of the dryads, the lady Zelkova who had selected Wren in the first place, spoke from her horse.

"Ahead of us is the Iron Thorn Bramble," she said. "We must go through. To go around the bramble would add a month to our journey. It is the haunt of disembodied chthonic spirits exiled from the golem peoples. These spirits will consume you if they can. So do not stray from the road. Do not touch the thorns. Do not eat any berry or fruit, nor drink any water you may find. If you have a weapon, keep it close to hand. Better yet, keep your wits about you."

Then Zelkova turned her mount and went into the Iron Thorn Bramble while her companion dryads stayed. A knight called out the names of his villages and commanded that they follow him. They did so, vanishing one-by-one into the brambles. Another knight did the same.

The third knight to call his charges was Sir Aethel. "Grunswald! Perswald! This way!" he shouted.

Leading from his horse, his men snaked behind him, including Ram and Wren. As with the other knights, the men followed Sir Aethel in a single line. No one wanted to be anywhere but in the middle of the road.

Once into the bramble, the sun seemed to diminish as the bramble branches reached up and over the road, forming a dark, thorny tunnel. The foliage seemed as if it were cast out of iron, certainly the sort of enchantment that golems might perform.

"Do you think the dryads keep the bramble from taking over the road?" Wren asked Ram. "Or does the bramble purposely lure and trap unwary travellers?"

Ram responded with his usual small grunt. He was used to responding this way to questions posed by his younger brother.

The men muttered quietly and gripped their weapons tightly. Ram held his great-grandfather's spearhead in a white-knuckled grip. Wren held the walking stick that he had carved on the second day of the march, but it felt so inconsequential in his hands. Others had hatches, knives, hunting spears, and other peasant weapons. Everyone was completely alert and extremely tense.

The road entered a light mist that appeared to be stuck on the iron thorns. The fog was clammy and grew thicker. Visibility dropped quickly. Soon, Wren had to squint to see Ram just in front of him. Just as the mist grew especially thick, Wren reached and held to Ram's pack. Someone grabbed his pack from behind, and he wondered if the entire levy was like this, hundreds of men forming a living chain.

The young man holding his pack pulled and pushed Wren's pack with a jerk. He laughed. Wren knew that snicker. It was Finch, once again expressing his casual cruelty.

The fog became denser, to the point that Wren couldn't see his own hands. It also darkened in color, turning a strange grey that looked unnatural and wrong to his eyes. The still air smelled fetid and felt colder. The feeling of something terrible just beyond their sight grew with every step. Finch ceased his game and held onto Wren's pack fearfully. He began breathing raggedly. For once Wren wasn't pleased at Finch's discomfort.

A rope of even darker fog, as thick as a man's thigh, seemed to push through the mist between Wren and Ram, as if it were attempting to split the brothers. It was so strange that it would find the small space between them. Thinking it might just be something in his eyes, something made more frightening by his fearful imagination, Wren blinked several times.

Strangely, Wren saw horrific visions with every blink. Closing his eyes was like opening them into an alternate dark universe. Yet these visions were of the same world around him, the dark iron brambles around them in constant, insane motion. The air was still, yet the plants moved as if a great wind rushed through. When his eyes were wide open, the plants were still again, completely motionless in reality.

Instead of blinking, Wren closed his eyes. The vision of the mad, rustling iron brambles continued unabated. Worse, Wren could see that the thick rope of dark fog between him and Ram was replaced by a bundle of thick, sickly-white vines, dotted with long iron thorns. On the vines he could see transparent veins, through which sap was visibly pumped like blood. Each individual vine moved on its own accord, squirming and writhing. Somehow he knew that the strange rope of wanted him. It hungered for him.

Horrified, Wren screamed. He opened his eyes. The vines turned to mist once again, but he knew what they really were. He let go of Ram, backed up, and collided with Finch. He tried to swing his walking stick at the rope of fog, but in his panic he fumbled, dropping his makeshift weapon. Then Wren slashed at the air barehanded, but his hands passed through the mist ineffectively. Time seemed to slow down as he realized his attempts would prove useless. Terror gripped his heart.

The rope of fog wrapped itself around Wren's midsection, the hidden thorns piercing through his tunic and skin. He screamed in agony. The vines pulled him away from the trail with their irresistible force.

The vines pulled Wren toward the thick bramble just feet away on the side of the road. This section was so thick that it seemed like an impenetrable wall. Then a horizontal line appeared along the bramble, splitting the wall of thorns. With a loud, creaking, crackling sound, the line widened into some kind of hideous mouth. Around it Wren could see the branches of the bramble pulling the mouth open. There was no evidence of any human hand in sight. With a snap, the rope of mist-cloaked vines pulled him in like an obscene tongue.

Wren redoubled his screams when he heard the crackle of the bramble shutting its mouth behind him.

"Wren! Wren! Where did you go?" Ram called in panic, his voice filled with fury. "Finch, what did you do to him? "

"Let me go! I didn't do anything. Something pulled into the brambles! Honest!" Finch yelled back.

"Wren! Wren! Where are you?" Ram shouted desperately.

At Ram's shout, Wren was flung to the ground. The rope of vines and its torturous thorns had expelled him. For a moment all he could think about was that the painful thorns were gone.

Then he realized that he was lying on bones of all types. He saw a skull next to his face. He felt in his heart that something was near, something really bad. A dark presence. He couldn't see it, but he was sure that something was watching him.

Somehow Wren felt the hunger of the dark presence. He knew that it wanted to consume him.

"Wren!" Ram shouted, as did others. "Wren! Where are you? Call out!"

Wren stopped screaming. He tried not to gasp. He even tried not to breathe. Perhaps if he was silent, whatever was here might not find him. Unless, of course, it was native to the mist, in which case it didn't matter, did it?

Fearing the worst, but needing to know the truth, Wren closed his eyes again.

Unencumbered by the blinding, warping mist, Wren could see everything clearly.

Just twenty feet from him, the brambles thickened into a dense patch that looked to be completely made of iron. Thorns here were each over a foot in length, with tips rusty from a green, slimy juice. The juice had to be poison. Just inside the branches of the bramble, he could see the dangling, eyeless remnant of some unfortunate animal.

If the mouth of the bramble had swallowed Wren, then this surely must be its gullet. Its prey would be digested here, much as a biscuit would be digested in Wren's stomach.

The idea that the brambles might be a living beast scraped at the edges of Wren's sanity. He screamed in shock, opening his eyes. He didn't want to see the truth anymore.

Eyes open, the monstrous gullet was gone, hidden in the mist. Sobbing, he backed away on all fours.

Another ghostly tentacle of mist emerged. It clutched his ankle, piercing his skins with its awful thorns. It pulled him through the mist and toward the gullet. Terrified, Wren wailed his fear.

"I heard him! Wren! I'm coming to get you," he heard Ram call. His brother sounded so very close. His heart rejoiced.

"There's nowhere to go! There's nothing to do!" Finch shouted.

"Let me go, Finch! Let me go, Ox! My brother is in there!" he heard Ram shout. Wren heard wrestling and grunts as his brother tried to break free.

"Help me!" Wren cried pitifully.

He felt the creature pulling him closer. He closed his eyes waiting for the terrible end. His blinks gave him quick glimpses, but eyes completely closed he could see it clear as day. Through his closed eyelids he could see the terrible digestive organ of the bramble. It was part of the bramble. This was a "bramble" in the same sense that the Dark Lord was a man. The branches were thick and knotting, almost muscled like a strong man's arms. Every branch moved, but the ones that did the most weren't made of iron, but colored like dark animal flesh. They would impale him with the longest thorns and consume his innards. White and black colored berries hung from a few branches, but only a few. It was a twisted mockery of berry patch.

One of the white and black berries blinked. Another turned its black spot to him.

Those weren't berries. Those were eyes: the eyes of its victims.

Wren thrashed frantically, trying to break free.

He felt his clothes snag on the bones covering the ground, and the tree-like monster's progress at devouring him halted. Oddly enough, many parts of his clothes snagged on the bones, as if they were holding him back.

All around him, Wren heard the bramble groan its frustration, pulling harder. The bramble's pulling on his ankle made him scream in agony. In the haze of pain, he wondered if his foot would be torn from its sockets.

Wren yanked his knife free from its sheath and tried to reach for his ankle. But his tunic was caught on too many bones, and he couldn't lean forward. In a moment of uncharacteristic clarity, he realized that what had given him just moments of extra time was now going to kill him.

More vines wrapped themselves around his ankles, legs, and arms. They tugged him harder. Wren screamed as the bones holding him back refused to let go. Distantly, he heard his brother scream in anguish along with him.

Then, he heard several inhuman voices cry behind him. The cries were those of dryads. Through his eyelids, he could see bright flares of blazing mystical light that left blotches in his eyes. It was as bright as looking up into the sun.

Through mouths unseen, the bramble howled in agony and let go. Someone reached out a hand from above and helped him to his feet. It was the lady dryad Zelkova. By the hand, she led him away at a run he could barely manage. He felt nauseous, sick, and weak. His vision through closed eyes faded, and he found himself blind again. He opened his eyes to see where he was going.

Even through the dense mist, Wren could see the three other dryads in the distance behind Zelkova, their weapons ablaze with bright power. By their sides were the weald hounds. Together with their pets, the dryads headed in the direction of the monstrous gullet.

Zelkova led Wren directly toward a wall of thorns through which he could see men. With a wave of her hand and unknown words spoken, she opened a channel through the dense thicket. Pulling him along, she dashed through the narrow tunnel and back to the column of mortal men.

"Run! All of you run! We'll hold the brambles long enough for you to get away!" she shouted.

Then Zelkova turned and ran back into the tunnel. The brambles closed behind her.

"Wren!" he heard Ram scream hoarsely from not far away.

"I'm here, Ram!" he said, gasping.

Wren was sweating and exhausted. He could barely stand. The many small punctures from the thorns stung. Looking down he saw his clothes covered with dots of his own blood.

"Wren!"

Ram pushed through the other young men to get to his brother, ignoring their complaints and cries. Then they were together again. Wren sagged, and Ram caught him before he completely collapsed.

"Run! Run!" a voice said.

Someone pushed them. Wren struggled for a moment, then Ram took him onto his back. Carrying Wren, Ram ran with the rest, away from the monster in the brambles.

CHAPTER 20

WREN

That night, even though they were past the Iron Thorn Bramble, the men huddled close to the fires and to each other. Extra sentries were set, and weapons were kept close at hand. Men even went in groups to a nearby stream. The sight of the Rainbow Mountains in the distance was a small comfort to them, but not enough.

Ram stayed close to Wren, holding their great-grandpa's spearhead as if it were a short sword. He stood watchful, peering beyond the fire for threatening evil.

Wren was ill. He felt nauseous, his skin clammy with sweat. The strength was gone from his limbs. He rested on his and Ram's cloaks next to a tree. His thoughts were jumbled, as if there was more than one voice in his head. He tried to tell his story, but forming coherent sentences and speaking loud enough for others to hear was hard.

The puncture wounds stung. They weren't bleeding anymore, but each one was a point of soreness. As if infected, the skin at the wounds was red and tight. None of the men were healers, so no one knew what to do.

Sir Aethel had talked briefly with Wren and Ram when they stopped. He said that he would ask the dryads for help with his wounds, but that was hours ago.

Finch, Sparrow, and Ox were not there. Ram had brandished great-grandpa's spearhead and threatened to kill them. Seeing the anger in eyes that were normally gentle, the trio moved away.

At first, the men wondered aloud if Wren would die. Injuries from rusted weapons were particularly nasty. The thorns of the bramble appeared to be made of iron, lending credence to Wren's imminent demise. Again, Ram intervened, stopping these public questions. He assured Wren that they would live together forever.

Wren wasn't so certain. He thought he was dying. In fact, death had a pleasant feeling about it. He could let go and not feel the pain in his wounds or in his memories anymore. He would be buried in cool, clean earth. Then a bramble would grow where he had died, his resting place a garden bed. He imagined that from where he would lie, a great briar patch would grow. It would be magnificent, for the bramble could grow to cover the world. This was truly a noble, giving ending.

When Ram tried to give him water, Wren refused. Instead, he quietly asked Ram to kill him. After all, the faster he died, the faster the bramble could grow.

To Wren's regret, Ram stepped back in horror. Ram put his hands over his ears. "Stop saying these horrible words. You're sick. I want you to get better," Ram said.

Wren decided to ask Finch to do it. He was certain that Finch would end him quickly enough. With his fever-quieted voice, he tried to ask Ram to bring their old nemesis.

Suddenly, one of the male dryads was standing next to Wren. Ram and the men around them jumped in shock. It was as if the branches next to Wren had been the dryad all along.

Quickly, the men got to their feet and bowed low to the dryad. He was an overlord, and to him such respect was due.

At night the dryad looked more human. In the light of candles and torches, the wood-grain-like patterning on his skin was impossible to see, and the thin vines that grew from its head impossible to differentiate from human hair. Yet at night when he did not move, he seemed to have the immobility of a planted tree.

The dryad had several leafy branches in his hands.

"Take off his tunic and pants. Leave his undergarments on," the dryad commanded.

Ram rushed to obey. Wren struggled against him weakly, but his clothes were quickly removed. Without any clothes, his scrawny nature was even more evident.

The dryad knelt beside the injured teen. He plucked a leaf from the branch and placed it on Wren's stomach, covering some of the injuries caused by the thorns. He repeated this with the rest of Wren's torso, and then his arms and legs. Soon every injury was covered. Then the forest lord instructed Ram to roll Wren over. Ram gently flipped his brother, and the dryad covered the injuries on Wren's other side. Then Ram rolled Wren onto his back again.

Finished with his task, the dryad stood up. He did this in a single, graceful motion. No mortal man was he to have grown stiff in the cold spring air by being in one position for a long time.

The dryad stood next to Wren for an hour, and then another. Not once did he move, not even seeming to breathe. Ram sat on a rock and waited patiently.

When Wren would close his eyes, the dryad transformed, becoming more like a bright, glowing tree than a man. The dryad's strange glow was brighter than a campfire. Wren could feel the mystic light entering his body through the leaves that covered his body. As it entered and passed through him, he could feel his wounds healing. His body was getting stronger again. Wren broke out in a sweat. An unpleasant-smelling green slime quickly covered his body.

"Bathe him in the stream," the dryad instructed Ram. "Do this not here but downstream from the camp, for that which he sweated was the poison of the bramble."

Ram bowed deeply and then picked up Wren. As his older brother carried him, Wren realized that he was feeling quite well. He still felt tired, but it was the good kind of tired that one felt after a long day.

The stream was biting cold, but Wren persevered. He and Ram washed and rubbed the green slime from Wren's body. As he was cleaned, Wren wondered what would happen to the fish and crawlers who breathed in the poison. Would it affect them?

Once Wren was clean, Ram helped him dry off by using his own cloak. It wasn't until he was nearly dry that Wren realized the dryad was there, possibly the whole time.

"I would talk to you, Wren of Perswald," the dryad said.

The dryad started walking. Wren, worn from his trials, nonetheless followed. Ram tagged along.

They followed the retreating figure of the dryad past the nervous sentries and into the dark of the forest. Curious, Wren closed his eyes and noticed he could see the dryad quite well. He couldn't see anything else, and he stumbled. He opened his eyes and continued with his normal vision, impaired as it was by the dark night.

Finally, the dryad stopped and faced them.

Wren and Ram approached cautiously. Dryads were immortal, and while they were normally beneficial overlords, they could sometimes turn malignant with capricious glee.

When the dryad didn't speak, Wren asked, "Milord?"

The dryad spoke. "I am Epiphron, mate of Zelkova, the one who summoned you for the levy. Wren, this evening I spoke to your liege, Sir Aethel. He said that this is not the first time that a monster has found you."

Wren thought back to Cora, the monster he had had known so briefly when he was still a child. "Yes, milord. There was a manticore. And cockatrice bones."

"When I look into you, as we saw in the village, I see a mortal with the gift of magic. I wonder what it is that you see in return," Epiphron said.

"What do you mean, milord?" asked Wren.

"By the accounting of your knight-magistrate, when the manticore was found, you thought it was just a normal little girl. Every other description is not so flattering," Epiphron said.

Wren wasn't certain what to say. Was he being tried? He was glad to have Ram's comforting presence.

"Do you ever see things that others cannot see?" asked Epiphron.

"I don't understand your question, milord," Wren said.

"I believe you do, young mortal. Tell me what you saw inside the Iron Thorn Bramble today."

Wren hesitated.

"It was a room inside a bramble," he said. "But with very long thorns and branches with muscles not unlike my brother's. Its berries were eyes. I knew that if it drew me in, it would tear me to pieces. Between the path and it were the bones of its victims."

Epiphron nodded. "You saw it then, with your own eyes? Through the mist?" he asked.

"Yes, milord."

"Then you have the mage-sight. And at such an uncommon level for someone untrained," Epiphron mused.

"Mage-sight, milord?"

"Every immortal is born with it, allowing us to see the mystical. We dryads have it. Golems have it. Sometimes mortals are born with it, but it is rare," Epiphron explained.

Wren clapped his hands with delight. Surely he was on the road to becoming a great wizard! Ram slapped his brother lightly on the back to express his joy.

"Don't celebrate just yet, mortal," the dryad reprimanded, "Mage-sight is a blessing and a curse. You could see the true nature of the bramble today, but it also blinded you to the monstrosity of the manticore. Just as saying the Adversary's name invites bad spirits, even worse things can find their way to you just because you looked in their direction and have mage-sight."

"Indeed, young Wren, mage-sight goes two ways. If you wish to have any control over the mage-sight, you must learn to use it to penetrate deception. You must also learn to ignore it and rely on the mundane eyes that the Creator gifted you with. Until then, you will attract more and more danger until the day that there aren't protectors on hand to rescue you."

"Can you teach me how to control the mage-sight?" Wren asked.

"No, I cannot. You are slated to be an apprentice of the Arch-Mage Eratea. She will teach you how to harness your magic power and properly control it, including your mage-sight. Unless the need were dire, if I were to teach you anything, it would be seen as presumptuous and beyond my place."

Wren summed up his courage and said, "Milord, we were attacked by a monster. If I could learn to control my mage-sight, perhaps I could help people avoid dangers."

The dryad's face went cold. "I will not step beyond my place and neither will you," he said.

"My apologies!" Wren said fearfully, bowing deeply. Ram followed suit. When they looked up, the dryad was gone.

DANIEL ROY GREENFELD

CHAPTER 21

RADNAG

The sun beat down on Abrog's head. Until they came to grips with Radnag's tribe, Abrog would keep his helmet off. He needed to be able to properly see and hear in order to pull this off. In his hands was a human's hunting bow, taken from their first village raid several weeks ago.

Crouching next to him, bow in hand and with hood shading his head was Gorgol, the best of the goblin hunters. Abrog still hadn't forgiven him for capturing Orbag, but he recognized his skills. This was a day where those skills were incredibly important.

Usually Abrog wore more armor, but for his self-appointed task today, he needed stealth. Instead, he wore a heavy quilted coat, one taken from the corpse of an armored human warrior that he had killed a week ago. The man's metal armor had lain over the coat, cushioning impacts. Abrog appreciated the design, even encouraging his tribe to layer their armor in the same way. His head was bare, for Abrog needed no hood from the bright sun on this bright, clear day. Unlike his tribe—his kin of the same original flesh and blood—his skin no longer burned, and, more importantly, his vision was not impaired.

In the shining light of day that nearly blinded the nocturnal goblin kind, they had managed to stealthily approach within striking distance of Radnag's hillside cave. Inside, goblins and hobgoblins would be sleeping, as would be most of the yearlings. Outside the cave, the gobs and hobs would be dozing in small dens. The only forces guarding the entrance were two sleepy looking goblins.

That wasn't where Abrog was attacking. Instead, he and Gorgol were stalking up the backside of Radnag's hill, intent on striking the guards from above. Two hundred paces behind them nearly the entire troop of Abrog's hunters waited.

As for the rest of Abrog's tribe, they were standing several hundred yards to the front of Radnag's cave, ready for Abrog's signal.

Abrog and Gorgol reached the summit of the hill. A clump of rocks was at the top, which Abrog and Gorgol approached carefully. This would be where the chimney from Radnag's cave would leak smoke to the world. It would also be where lookouts were posted. While Abrog and Gorgol didn't see any movement there, that could mean the lookouts were just being careful.

Less than a dozen feet away from the rocks, Abrog and Gorgol heard a chirp. They froze. A little gob scrambled up onto a waist-high rock. He squinted at them through the bright light of day.

Abrog's bow came forward of its own accord. At this range he couldn't miss. He pulled back the string to his ear, getting ready to fire. But then he stopped.

He remembered poor Orbag who didn't live her life: his beloved sister who was killed by his own kind, who didn't have the chance to grow up into a hobgoblin. She was just another victim in the brutally short life of most of his kind.

Try as he might, Abrog couldn't take the shot.

Gorgol loosed his own bow. For the briefest of moments Abrog felt absolute panic for the gob, but the arrow flashed past it. The missile hammered into the face of a sleepy-faced adult goblin peering over one of the rocks. The hapless goblin pitched backwards out of sight without a sound. The child goblin squeaked, hopped off its perch, and vanished into a small cleft between the rocks.

Broken free of his reverie, Abrog ran forward and leapt onto one of the rocks. In the shadow of the rocky cleft around the chimney hole, five goblins of Radnag's tribe lounged. Only the gob had noticed Abrog and Gorgol's approach, but now they all knew that the enemy was in their midst.

Abrog knew that hesitation would mean failure and likely death. Hoping that Gorgol was with him, he loosed his arrow at the closest goblin of Radnag's tribe. Then Abrog flung aside his bow, pulled his axe from his belt, and jumped into the midst of the enemy.

Abrog landed in the space between three of the five remaining goblin guards. As he descended, he brought down his axe onto the head of the guard. The guard collapsed, almost taking the axe from Abrog's hand.

One down. That left four for him and Gorgol to kill.

With a yank, Abrog freed his weapon and buried it into another victim's ribcage. It wasn't an immediately killing blow, but Abrog was certain the goblin would be too occupied by his wound to do anything else. The goblin howled pitifully as it began to crumple.

Three enemy goblins left.

Still on the ground, one of the goblin guards reached for his spear. Abrog was going to have none of that. As he wrenched his axe clear, he stepped forward and kicked the spear-goblin. This knocked the goblin sprawling; Abrog was on him in a moment. Two quick chops ended the spear-goblin.

Two enemy goblins left.

Abrog looked around. Another goblin was writhing on the ground, with Gorgol's hunting blanket covering his head and a knife in his gut.

One goblin left.

Abrog heard the clash of weapons. He saw Gorgol trading desperate blows with the last goblin. Both weary and out of breath, they fought but were an even match. The goblin saw out of the corner of his eye that Abrog had finished off the others. In a panic, he jumped back, trying to scramble backwards over the rocks.

Abrog threw his weapon. As a goblin's melee axe it wasn't expressly designed for this kind of use, but the range was close. Abrog had spent the time needed to get good at throwing it. He had practiced his technique with endless patience, for who knew when an occasion like this might arise. The axe buried itself in the goblin's back. The goblin shrieked in pain, tumbling off the rocks and onto the ground on the other side. Abrog could tell that the goblin was dying, for his groans were fading by the second.

"The gob that first saw us, where did he go?" Abrog demanded. He gasped for air. Fighting was hard work!

"Smart little critter ran off. I've seen that happen," Gorgol said, smiling at his private, little joke that he knew only Abrog would understand. "What now boss?"

"I'm not hearing any alarm raise. Fortune is on our side. We stick with the plan. You know what to do," Abrog said.

Abrog climbed over the rocks to the dying goblin. He wrenched the axe from his chest and then left his victim in peace. He circled around the rocks to where he had dropped his bow. He picked up the bow and then headed toward the edge of the cliff above Radnag's cave. So far, his plan to force Radnag into a new type of conflict was working. It was a new form of warfare.

"Are you sure you don't want to block the chimney?" Gorgol asked.

"No. We want Radnag to stay in her filthy hole, not come out," Abrog said.

Twenty paces later, Abrog was looking down on the bald heads of two goblin guards assigned to watch the entry to Radnag's lair. They were stretching and yawning, sleepy in the middle of day. If they had been in his tribe, he would have had them flayed alive for not hearing the fight above.

Fortunately for them, the justice he was going to mete out would be a lot quicker. He knocked an arrow, pulled the string back to his cheek, and carefully took aim. Gorgol caught up with him and readied his own arrow.

Abrog took in a deep breath. Then he yelled at the top of his lungs. "FORWARD!" he said, shooting arrows with Gorgol.

Abrog's arrow struck one of the goblin guards in the leg. Gorgol's arrow went right into the throat of his companion guard. Both collapsed, one screaming, one silent. The injured goblin crawled frantically into the cave.

From within the forest, Abrog heard the answering roar of his tribe. For a few moments he could see nothing in the woods where they hid from the light of day. Then his tribe emerged. First there were a few of them, and then a crowd of a hundred goblins and a few dozen hobgoblins emerged from the trees and brush. They were all covered with blankets and hoods to protect against the hated sun. They stumbled forward. They were half-blinded by the light, but forward they came.

A band of twenty goblin archers emerged from a point closer to the side of the hill. Half of their weapons had been taken from dead humans on previous raids. They ran up the hill to join Abrog and Gorgol.

When the bulk of his force was fifty paces from the cave entrance, Abrog bellowed his next command. "Halt!" he said. Goblin and hobgoblin came crashing to a stop. They carried as many ranged weapons as they could find: rocks, javelins, axes, throwing clubs, and bows. There were never enough archers, even with the addition of the bows collected in the human villages.

It didn't matter, though. They would be enough to keep Radnag's tribe bottled up long enough for the hunters to do their work.

Seeing the troops in place in front of and above the cave entrance, Abrog nodded at Gorgol. The smaller goblin went down the backside of the hill. Staying just out of bowshot of the lair's entrance, Abrog went to where the bulk of his minions waited.

Just as he reached the bottom of the hill, Abrog watched a half-dozen enemy goblins run out of the cave, shields held high. His own archers responded with arrows from above and in front. Hit from both angles, all the enemy goblins were down in seconds, dead or injured. Abrog grinned at how well his tribe was doing against the old enemy, Radnag.

His own tribe cheered him as he rejoined them. By now he had enough successes to have built some trust with them. This plan seemed to be winning, and goblins liked to follow winners.

"We're doing great!" Abrog said to his minions. "Don't stop yet. There may be more. Kill anything that tries to leave that cave!"

They waited for an hour as the sun moved across the sky. Abrog's tribe jeered Radnag and her tribe. He let them have their fun. Normally this was sleeping time, not fighting time. His tribe might be annoyed by the results of this very different kind of raid, and he wanted to keep them happy. Still, with an iron fist, he didn't let them break ranks to smash everything in sight. When a goblin or hobgoblin became too eager, he would leap to beat and kick it back into line.

This particular raid followed a new concept. He was attacking Radnag in a way that she couldn't counter, one that didn't attack her directly.

Abrog heard Gorgol's horn. That was the signal that Gorgol and the other hunters had done their work. It was time to go.

"Time to go home!" Abrog ordered.

He and his tribe melted back into the forest, heading to their own cave.

Most of his tribe was exhausted, but Abrog had kept a third of the tribe back at the cave during the raid. As evening fell, they took up alerted guard over their cave and territory. In case Radnag were to counter-attack, the rested third would be the first line of defense. The tired majority of the tribe relaxed on top of the hill in rough shelters. The human slaves taken in previous raids had built these temporary shelters for the tribe.

Abrog wasn't entirely certain whether Radnag would counter. There was a good chance she would laugh off his attack, calling it a favor.

Unlike the normal assaults of chieftains upon other tribes, his assault hadn't been designed to lure out the enemy tribe from their cave. He hadn't attempted to force them out of their lair or even smash up their domain. A few taunts, then a retreat was all that Radnag had seen him do.

While Abrog was bottling up Radnag's tribe, his hunters had captured dozens of gobs and hobs in blankets and nets. They had dug up scores of eggs that had been laid by Radnag's hobgoblins in loose dirt, sticking them into packs. All the youngest had been taken from Radnag's tribe. Abrog was certain that Radnag would be happy that the 'pests' had been cleaned out.

Abrog smiled as the hunters released the gobs and hobs into the old great cave room in the cave. They joined all the other gobs and hobs his tribe under his orders had forced into the space. His little beasts screamed and wailed at the new beasts. At Abrog's word, human slaves brought in baskets of food, dumping their contents on the cave floor for the little ones. The caterwauling of the young ceased as en masse they plunged into the food that they so craved. Soon he would let the larger ones out, but for now the cave was their new home. This was how it now was to be for all the other gobs and hobs in the tribe.

The eggs stolen from Radnag's tribe were placed in shallow dirt in other rooms, alongside those laid there by his own tribe's hobgoblins. The hatchlings of both tribes would begin their life as Abrog's minions.

DANIEL ROY GREENFELD

Thanks to this raid alone, his tribe had doubled in size. His domain was crawling with youngsters. They were annoying, often considered pests, normally eaten as food. Yet he had the foresight to realize that if he could keep the young alive and safe, his tribe would overwhelm the other tribes.

More tribe members meant more trained hunters, which in turn meant more raids on humans for food and for slaves to make more food.

It was just a matter of numbers, really.

Abrog left the raucous youngsters to their meal. He trudged through hallways filled with exhausted hobgoblins and goblins, making his way out of the cave. Outside, in the evening air, the rested third of his tribe kept careful guard just in case Radnag launched a counter attack. Abrog was tired, but he joined them in their duty.

He knew that the odds were that Radnag wasn't going to do anything tonight, tomorrow, or ever. Taking the youngsters would be seen as a favor, even mocked. He imagined her laughing at him, but he knew she wouldn't be laughing about the future he had stolen from her. The youths he had stolen from their tribe would return one day, with him at their command.

DANIEL ROY GREENFELD

CHAPTER 22

ROCKSLIDE PASS

For most of the march from the Black Thorn Bramble, Wren, Ram, and the others followed the edge of the Rainbow Mountains. Passes were few and well guarded. Depending on the season, some were closed to all traffic.

As they approached the entrance to the pass, the young men and their leaders could see the gate from miles away. The posts of the gates were giant statues of dryads, large enough that their genders—male and female—could be determined.

The approach to the mountains emerged from the forest and began to wind upwards. It was a steep road. Even after weeks on the march, the men found themselves tiring easily. For Wren, it was a nightmare. He gasped and choked for air. His legs burned, and his back hurt.

Ram tried to help. He encouraged Wren with small grunts. He pushed. He pulled. He even carried him for a mile before even his mighty thews trembled with fatigue. His months of carrying large piles of wood back at home had given him endurance. Accustomed to the easy chores, Wren did not have any of Ram's endurance.

They fell behind the column. Shadows lengthened as the day turned into evening. Wren's stomach rumbled constantly. He felt his strength draining away. It became too much, and he sat down trying to find his wind. Ram pulled his arm and grunted for him to get up. Hungry and deeply tired, Wren waved him off.

Ram backed away and stood nearby. He waited patiently. The sun started to set, turning the sky into a brilliant world of orange and red hues.

Wren didn't notice any of this. He stared at the ground, at the grains of dirt. He was exhausted. Dejected. The journey had been hard, and now his body felt finished.

Ram finally spoke. "Look, a horseman is coming," he said.

Wren looked up. Coming from higher on the mountain was Sir Aethel, riding alone and without a retainer. He was on a riding nag, and he led a pack mule. Wren stood up as his liege approached. He felt fear in his heart. The knight would probably be very angry.

Sir Aethel stopped in front of the brothers.

"Onto the mule," the knight said, annoyance in his voice.

Ram helped Wren onto the mule while the knight watched. Wren had never been on a mount before, and he seemed terribly high. He felt like he was going to slide right off, and he marveled at how easily the knight sat on his horse.

"Lash your brother to the mule, or he'll fall off. Then the dryads will be angry for losing their prize," the knight said angrily, obviously trying to keep his temper in check.

Ram took a coil of rope off the mule. He began to lash Wren firmly to the packsaddle.

Wren felt a mix of pride and shame. The knight had called him the "dryad's prize," meaning that the dryads had probably ordered Sir Aethel to fetch the brothers. However, being tied to a mule because he couldn't keep up was going to make him look weak in front of his peers. Cautiously, he avoided vocalizing the giant sigh he wanted to give. No doubt the knight would not be amused.

Finally satisfied with Ram's handiwork, Sir Aethel walked his horse up the hill. Ram followed behind, leading Wren's mule. As they progressed up the hill, Wren felt relief knowing that they would join the others for the evening.

The gate to Rockslide Pass was enormous. Combined with the door of the gate, the statues blocked the entrance.

The statue posts were hundreds of feet tall. Carved in the likeness of a Dryad king and queen, Wren wondered who had done the work. Dryads were not normally known for their stonecraft, so this had to have been done by someone or something else. Perhaps the gate was made by golems in ancient times, craftsmen of one of the lost races, or even shaped by the hands of the three craft-working gods themselves!

The door of the gate only came up to the knees of the statues, yet it too was impressive. Made of bronze that refused to tarnish, it gleamed in the light of the glowing lamps held by the hands of the statues. Such a raw display of magic was unknown to Wren and rare in his small world, even though he had heard that even more fantastical things lay ahead in the Valley of Wizardry.

As they came closer, Wren noticed that the legs of the statues had arrow slits near the base, and windows near the top of the gate. In the light of the lamps, he could see that on the top of the bronze door was a walkway, and men, or perhaps even dryads, looked down on Wren, Ram, and Sir Aethel.

The great door was nearly shut. Where it remained open, a trio of male dryads stood, along with twenty men. All of them, immortal and mortal, were armed with bows and gleaming shirts of mail.

Wren closed his eyes, trying to look with his mage-sight. There was darkness at first, and then he saw light. The light grew, and he saw that the gate itself emitted it. The bronze door gleamed, and the statues shined. Every moment they seemed to become brighter.

In his peripheral vision he saw something move. He gazed upwards. The statues were turning their heads, staring down at him, following as he came closer to them. The gate blazed with terrible brightness, so loud that it seared into his skull.

With a shout, Wren wrenched his eyes open.

The soothing coolness of normal sight night felt incredible. It was as if his eyes had been on fire and then doused with cool, refreshing water.

The statues were as stone, in the same position they had been for thousands of years.

He turned his own gaze downward toward the dryads. They looked at him with the placid calmness of a still pond.

"Zelkova and her mate Epiphron were correct," murmured one of the dryads to another. "This one has great talent. Eratea will be pleased."

Exhausted as he was, Wren found heart in the compliment. He might be arriving tied to a mule, but he would be leaving under different means.

"You may pass," said a dryad. He made a motion. The men standing with him parted to let them pass.

Sir Aethel led Wren and Ram through the guards and then through the gate. The dryads and men followed. The gate closed behind them, the sound of it a deep, vibrating bass note like the sound made by an immense drum.

On the other side of the gate, there were a number of three- and four-story stone buildings with thatched roofs placed right up against the rock face of the pass. Built for defense against an enemy coming through the pass, they lacked windows on the first two levels.

Sir Aethel led the brothers towards one of them, while the gate guards went in another direction. As they arrived, Wren heard laughter and singing coming from inside.

"Untie your brother," Sir Aethel said.

Ram, more capable with knots then speech, quickly freed Wren. He helped him down off the mule.

"Come here, boy," Sir Aethel said.

Wren nervously approached. If he wanted to, by his rights Sir Aethel could have him whipped, for he was a knight and Wren was merely a serf.

Sir Aethel looked down at him from his horse. "The dryads really want you, boy," he said. "More than me. More than even your entire village. So next time the road gets rough, I'll see you through. In return, when you get to the Tower of Sorcery, you'll remember the favor I've done for you. Aye?"

"Aye, milord," Wren answered.

"You are dismissed."

Wren and Ram bowed, turned and entered the building to join their comrades.

The next day was less challenging for Wren. No longer were they going up a slope for mile after mile. Instead, they made their way through the level ground of Rockslide Pass.

The gate they had passed through last night warded one end of Rockslide Pass. This was one of the few entrances to the Valley of Wizardry. The Rainbow Mountains were said to be the bodies of immortal rainbow giants slain by gods in a much earlier age. The giants might be dead, but their spirits were still bitter about his defeat. When they sensed anyone trespassing their rocky corpses, they would shake and send great slides of rock down his slopes to crush and destroy. Great enchantments kept the angry mountain spirits asleep, so the pass was of no danger. However, in times of danger, the spirit of the dead giants could be awoken. The cranky mountains would shake and tremble, burying any unfortunate enough to attempt a crossing.

Rockslide Pass was miles long, so long that it would take two days to march through. The as-yet-trained army stopped for the evening halfway through the pass. Most of the men slept under the stars. The knights slept in a traveler's inn strategically placed in the middle of the pass for optimum business.

Over a campfire, a quick-witted young man told a tale about Rockslide Pass. Crow, noted for his storytelling, was from the neighboring village of Grunswald.

Wren and Ram sat around the campfire with fellow villagers from both Perswald and Grunswald. He wasn't happy sitting with Finch, Sparrow, and Ox, but what choice did he have? Even without minstrel training, Crow's stories were magnificent to hear.

Crow began in a low voice. "Ages ago," he said, "before even the Dark Lord walked the world, the armies of the Dominator sieged the Tower of Sorcery. The dryads summoned all to their aid, including the mighty king Koth. Koth! So wise was he that the dryads appointed him as their council. So accomplished a general was he that the golems made him their marshal.

Crow flung his arms into the air and shouted into the night. "King Koth! One of the greatest men to ever walk the world!" he said.

Wren and others cheered King Koth. Crow grinned.

"Aye, King Koth marched to the defense of the Tower of Sorcery. He assembled a great army from the lowlands. His soldiers he garbed in gleaming armor and gave them wondrous weapons. They affirmed his right to lead, and lead them he did!

"To Rockslide Pass, Koth marched his army. No quicker route lay between King Koth's land and the defense of the dryad overlords. A man of honor, King Koth raced as quickly as he could to protect his lieges.

"Koth and his army came in the middle of spring, not unlike ourselves. In similar fashion to our own, they camped the night away not far from where we sit around this campfire. They too dined on poultry and mutton, washing down their meal with fresh spring water. Dare I say they even listened to a magnificent teller of tales that night?"

Crow grinned. The men laughed.

"AND YET!" Crow shouted the men into quiet. "There was a difference. A terrible, terrible difference."

"The night that they slept in the pass was the night of the first, most fiercest thunderstorm of the year." Crow nodded and sneered. "Like us, they were unprepared for such a storm.

"Lightning blazed so that the night was turned into day. Thunder deafened men and killed the horses. Rain drowned the goats and sheep. And the wind knocked down tents.

"The men scrambled to find whatever cover that could be found. Unlike today, no massive boulders littered the pass. No overhangs were to be crouched under, no lee to protect against the wind. The walls of the pass channeled the wind, rain, and lightning.

"All that stood between the men and the storm were a few trees, not unlike the ones over there. Everyone ran to the trees and begged the gods to protect them. Everyone hid under the tree limbs, huddling together like lambs in a storm.

"In the midst of the chaos of the storm and the panic of the men, King Koth attempted to gather the men. Alas, most were too addled by the elements, and ignored his commands. A few men, the boldest men, left the useless shelter of tree branches to stand by their lord.

"As soon as a hundred men joined Koth, the torment of the storm redoubled. Lightning from the sky attempted to tear apart the mountains. Thunder crashed in the air, men were deafened, and the ground began to shake.

"The men standing by Koth stood strong and silent, but those who did not heed his command cried in fear. They wailed like children. They begged the gods like dogs. Koth commanded them to join him once more, but his wayward troops held onto each other like a toddler clutches his mother's skirts."

Crow's voice, which had become louder and more dramatic, dropped into tenderness. "Alas, the men who did not listen to Koth did not realize that tonight they were being judged by the spirits of rainbow giants themselves. Little did they know that the storm was the doing of the dead giants. The giants respected King Koth and didn't want him to march into battle with troops who did not trust the great king."

Now Crow pointed a finger beyond the campfire and shouted, "Do you see that boulder there? That was the first stone cast by the mighty giants. It landed on fifty men trying to hide under an oak, crushing both tree and treachery flat.

"Boom! Another boulder was cast, crushing a hundred men this time! BOOM! Another tossed down from mountain high, smashing even more!

"BOOM! BOOM! BOOM!" Crow shouted. Then he stopped for a minute. Warily he looked at his comrades. "Look all around you. Look! See the boulders? There are a hundred of them! They are the tombs of thousands of Koth's men, destroyed by the Mountain Giants for failing the tests of courage and loyalty!

"Those that lived...those that stood by Koth in the storm... they became 'Koth's Hundred.' They stood against the tide of the Dominator. They turned back the end of the world."

Crow looked several men in the face, including Wren. "What about us?" he asked. "When our lieges call, when the dryads command, will we cower like lambs in a storm, or stand like men?"

The men roared their answer. Wren roared with them, but deep inside he feared that he knew what he would have done.

CHAPTER 23

DECISION

Gone was Annathea's old, wide-brimmed brown hat, replaced by a black-brimmed hat with a silver band. She had purchased it in the Marble Nation. The style of the hat was exotic in a way that she thought was quite pretty.

She wore a brown riding dress to hide the road dust. Black showed dirt stains and marks more quickly. Over it was a leather jerkin with long sleeves, with slivers of iron sewn along the length of each arm. This offered a bit of protection against slashes and cuts, but it was useless against arrows and spears.

She was taller now. Not long after she had struck out with her own caravan, a growth spurt put her over the head of Sir Oliver. At eighteen, she was now certainly an inch taller than her mother, which pleased her to no end.

DANIEL ROY GREENFELD

Mounted on Star, her horse, Annathea watched her caravan as it slowly exited the fortified gate of the mountain pass. The gate, like all golem structures, was squat and powerful, much stronger than any human construction. Her caravan seemed small and insignificant in its shadow.

Small my caravan might be, but it is all mine, she thought. *Well, the debt for it is mine, anyway.*

She had commanded the caravan for a year now, having taken half of her parents' caravan just two years after the Invulnerable Overlord's judgment. Of course, in nine more years she would have to share the caravan, or the debt of it, with her betrothed, young Durian Blue Branch. Still, for now it was her caravan.

Advised and guided by her uncle and aunt, Sir Oliver and Lady Harrieta, she had taken the caravan across the Granite Nation of golems and into the Marble Nation. They had done well there, and were now heading back home to the City-State of the Invulnerable Overlord. The plan was to make it back by the yearly city fair, since that would be a great time for business. Returning would also mean seeing her parents, possible some of her siblings as well.

Over the months away from her parents, the irritation she had felt towards her mother had faded into a more clinical observation. Her mother, Samantha Long Reach, had been spiteful and arrogant. For most of her life, she had never really demonstrated confidence in her. However uncomfortable that made Annathea feel, it had been her mother's method of instruction. Indeed, when times had been tough this past year, her ability to overcome problems had been forged in trying to overcome her mother's disdain. She resented her mother, and would feel that way until the end of her life, but now she could acknowledge that her mother's method of upbringing had worked.

Well, if there was anything she was going to do with her life, it was to raise her own children in a more encouraging manner.

In the meantime, she had a lot of hard work to do. Her task of leading the caravan wasn't easy, and it was often dangerous. The danger was more prevalent because of the horses and oxen around their heavy wagons that were dangerously large animals. She wasn't worried about the bandits or the mythical goblins that were said to infest some parts of the land.

There hadn't been serious trouble from bandits since she was a little girl. As for goblins, they had been nothing but a mere rumor for hundreds of years. If not for the memories of living golems who fought goblins in the days of the Dark Lord, goblins would have faded into myth.

Once the caravan was past the gate, she kicked her mount, Star, into a trot and rode the length of it. No faster than a man's walking pace did it move, so her journey was quite brief. At the very front of the caravan,

Sir Oliver rode his own horse, talking to the lead wagon driver. They looked at the storm clouds ahead. When she arrived, the two men turned to look at her, their liege.

"We're not going to make it to the Four Fathers' Bridge before the snow melts really hit it, will we?" Annathea asked. Every spring the local rains and melting snow on distant mountains combined to raise the rivers. While the golems had once built dams to control the inevitable flooding, just a year ago one of these had collapsed. That meant that during flood season, many of the bridges crossing this river would be unusable.

The lead wagon driver doffed his hat. He said, "Milady, the chances are slim. If we don't make it in time, the bridge will be flooded for a month. We'll miss the fair."

"What are the chances that the golems fixed the dam already?" she asked.

"Hard to say, milady," the driver said. "Even if they started right after we passed through on the way to the Marble Nation, fixing a collapsed dam is a huge amount of work even for them. They might not have completed repairs."

Annathea nodded. "Any alternatives?" she asked.

"We can go west, but that puts us at the edge of the war with the dryads," Sir Oliver said. "The caravan could get commandeered or even attacked. Best that we keep our distance."

"East puts us in the Old Lands, which are said to be haunted," said the driver, making the fist-like rock sign of the golems to ward off evil.

"The Old Lands have farms and valleys like the rest of the Granite Nation," Sir Oliver said, rolling his eyes. "If landed peasants can work the fields, and if landed nobles can collect a tax, then we can pass through."

"And the hauntings? And ghosts?" asked the driver.

"We'll double-tithe at every temple from here until there," Annathea said. "And we'll keep our guard up in case it's not ghosts to be worried about. How does that sound?"

They both looked at the lead driver. He nodded slowly. "Well, the men won't be happy, but they'll do it, milady," he said.

"So let it be done," said Annathea. "At the next crossroad we'll bear right, toward the East."

CHAPTER 24

TRAVELING INN

"That one will put to sleep even the most ravenous of bulls, milady. All you must do is slip a drop into a person's drink, and they will fall to a gentle sleep in minutes."

Annathea looked at the vial dubiously. She only had minutes before Harrieta caught up to her. She loved her aunt and uncle, but she really wanted some freedom from their near-constant chaperoning. It was so frustrating. She had run the caravan for well over a year and was still treated like a little girl.

Well, if this potion wasn't worthless colored water, she might be able to steal out to that young, handsome Officer of the Clerk while her guardians slept. He had caught her eye. Through questions she had cautiously asked of local merchants about the community here, she knew that he was noble and unattached to any woman. She found this out carefully so as not to arouse

DANIEL ROY GREENFELD

suspicion. She wasn't about to give up her virtue, but she longed for unchaperoned male company. By all the gods, she was eighteen and capable of good judgment!

Sighing internally, Annathea wished that Harrieta were the type to willingly drink strong liquor. Instead, she had to rely on subterfuge, in this case with what might be a dangerous magic potion.

"How do I know this will work?" Annathea asked.

"I crafted this myself! The recipe comes from my grandmother, who learned it from her grandmother, who learned it of old," the old, wizened potion dealer stated virtuously.

"What do you mean by 'of old'?" Annathea asked.

"What?"

"You heard me," Annathea said. "Explain this 'old' of which you speak."

The potion dealer drew herself up and said with utmost importance, "I cannot say."

"You don't know."

"I mean that my grandmother's grandmother had this recipe, and I do not know its source."

Annathea shrugged. That was as good an answer as any. She reached into her purse to find the right coin. Just then, there was a loud crash next to the potion dealer's stall.

She peeked out and saw several of her grooms in a market-yard brawl with some of the local laborers. Others were already starting to join in the melee. Whatever reason had started the mess was forgotten in the escalating conflict.

This wasn't good. Picking a fight with the locals always caused trouble, and picking a fight at the Crossroads Traveling Inn was worse. This could sour her travels on this side of the Granite Nation for years to come. The inn was the size of a keep, complete with 10-foot-high log walls protecting a space large enough for three caravans of their size to spend the night. It served as the center point of commerce and travel in this region. If this fight got out of hand, she could be barred for life.

She had to end the fight quickly and do it in a way that didn't turn the locals against her. Her sword was too lethal unsheathed and not effective enough in its scabbard. She looked around and saw a woodcarver's stall, complete with walking sticks. That would have to do.

Dodging a pair of men swinging haymakers at each other, she ran to the woodcarver. She yanked her sword and scabbard from her belt, handing them to the craftsman gawking at the brawl. Then she snatched up a stout-looking, carved walking stick just a little shorter than her nose. He protested, and she shouted, "I'm leaving my sword here as collateral!"

She turned and waded into the melee, shouting in her loudest command voice. "Cease this fighting!" she said.

Annathea was purposefully indiscriminate, hitting her own vassals as readily as she did men she didn't know. Not knowing how to use the stick like a staff, she wielded it like a spear, jabbing it hard into the gut of her opponents. She avoided face and neck thrusts, not wanting to really hurt her targets.

Men collapsed, gasping in agony. On both sides, most of the brawlers noticed her assaults and moved away, not noticing that they were retreating as a group.

One man on her flank grabbed a bucket. He darted in to smash it on her head. However, Annathea had been trained quite well by her uncle, Sir Oliver. As she fought, she watched the shadows on the ground and was aware of her attacker. She skipped forward as the bucket plunged through the space where her head had been. Then she whirled around. With her walking stick weapon, she whipped her attacker cruelly across the buttocks.

"Stop fighting!" Annathea commanded again, pointing the stick at the brawlers.

A couple of men scrambled at her, swinging merchandise wildly. The lead wagon driver tackled one of them. The other was trying to brain her with what looked like the leg of a broken chair.

The man was large and stocky, with a battered face that showed years of brawling. His swing was lightning fast. Annathea took a practiced half step back and let his wild swing flash past her. She tapped him hard on top of the head with her stick and declared angrily, "How dare you attack a lady?"

The blow didn't begin to slow him down, but her question did. Striking at a noble, even a trader-noble, was a death sentence in golem lands. He dropped his makeshift weapon, dropped to his knees and pleaded, "Milady, I'm sorry! I meant nothing by it!"

Others heard the tough-looking brawler's statement, and the fighting utterly ceased.

Annathea knew she had to reinforce her dominance. She rested her walking stick on his shoulder and asked, "Why shouldn't I have the wardens chop off your head?"

"Milady…I have a family. Children!" he begged.

"Well then, see to it that your children are raised with better manners than yourself," Annathea ordered. She then lifted her weapon.

The wardens of the inn finally made their appearance, pushing and shoving the men further apart. Annathea could not help but notice that they were shoving her men with more force than they did the locals. She sighed, for that was the way of things. It was time for her to intervene.

"You there!" she called, pointing at a warden. Then, with as much command as she could muster, she demanded, "How dare you strike my servant?"

The wardens toned down their behavior. Her men sidled over to her.

"It's going to be unpleasant if we stay here much longer," one of her grooms said quietly, a bruise welling up around his eye. Annathea, gazing at the look in the eyes of the local laborers and wardens, could not help but agree.

She cursed her luck. Her one chance in a while to have anything besides a lonely night had been dashed.

"We're leaving at dawn, tomorrow," Annathea said loudly, making certain that all witnesses heard her. "We'll make preparations tonight."

She walked over to the walking stick vendor. Then she exchanged her improvised weapon for her sword with the speechless merchant. She nodded curtly at the wardens and led her men out of the Inn's courtyard. Right outside was where her caravan had encamped.

At the edge of the encampment, Sir Oliver raised an eyebrow at the sight of Annathea and the good number of their crew walking out of the courtyard.

"There was a big fight inside," she said. "It's settled now, but we're leaving tomorrow. Please see that we are ready at first light in the morning."

Sir Oliver nodded and began to shout instructions. The men scrambled to obey him, but many thanked her before attending to their appointed tasks. The way she had resolved the fight proved once more that she was very much a lady noble-trader and worthy of their respect.

While Sir Oliver and the crew went about their work, she walked over to her wagon. She carefully checked her sword and its scabbard in case the merchant had done anything. Then she checked the two weapons she normally left on the cart, her bow and spear. After that, she went over to the horses grazing nearby. She found Star, her horse, petted him, and fed him an apple. During all of this, she remained cool and collected, aloof from her staff's rants about the people of the inn.

During all of this, what Annathea really wanted to do was bang her head against the wooden slats of her wagon. Alas, the need for decorum presided. Part of why the crew of the caravan followed her so willingly was her constant display of grace. Acting out her frustration would weaken her position.

Her mother had taught her that leadership was hard, doubly so for women. A noble male could show such weakness, even throw tantrums. For a noble lady to do so would make her seem childish and unworthy of respect.

"I've put up a light guard," Sir Oliver said that evening as he walked up to Harrieta and Annathea. The two women were sitting on wooden folding chairs just inside their circled caravan, still inside the walls of the Crossroads Traveling Inn. Harrieta was knitting, and Annathea was chewing on a blade of grass.

"I guess it's necessary," said Annathea dourly. "It's unfortunate that the fight began so early during our stay. We'll have to leave in the morning."

"I wish I had more time to find new fabrics. How am I supposed to make you a new dress for the fair if I don't have new fabric?" sulked Harrieta.

"What started the fight, anyway? Last time we were here there weren't any problems," said Sir Oliver.

Annathea sighed. "Last time the people here didn't know that I was actually in command," she said. "They assumed that you were the boss, Sir Oliver. They gave our men trouble for it, and our men took exception," she said.

She traded looks with Sir Oliver. He shrugged, saying, "I expected this to happen."

"How do I make it so our men aren't mocked because their leader is a woman? Must I declare you steward of my caravan?"

Sir Oliver laughed. "I'm your foreman, your chief retainer. I don't want to be anything else. You have to learn how to deal with this on your own," he said.

"It's so frustrating," Annathea complained. "I can lead as well as any man. Our men are okay with me. But it's the outsiders that cause problems."

"This is going to be something that you'll have to live with your entire life," Harrieta observed.

"You aren't far from the truth, damn it all," Annathea said. "The problem is that your reluctance to take the title and role means that we have problems we could otherwise avoid."

"A lady does not use foul language," Harrieta said stiffly.

"I'm sorry, Aunt Harrieta. I'm just frustrated."

"A fight might have broken out regardless of your gender," Sir Oliver observed. "Sometimes people just like to pick fights. These things just happen from time to time."

Annathea nodded. She had certainly picked arguments with her siblings and parents. When she was younger, she had even picked fights with servants. Her fights were usually over trivial things, she thought. She could well understand this happening. More importantly, complaining about the problem wasn't going to fix it. She simply had to get better at mitigating the aftereffects of a brawl.

"Someone's coming from the courtyard!" a sentry called out to them.

Annathea, Oliver, and Harrieta turned to see a heavyset man walk into the caravan circle. A fringe of floppy hair surrounded the man's shiny bald head. His clothes were a clean set of well-made trousers and a matching tunic. Instead of boots, he wore shoes. They recognized him as being the son of the inn's aged owner—the man who actually ran the place. Even though as a commoner his status was less than their own, they stood up to greet him, as a sign of respect.

In the innkeeper's hands was a tray holding a bottle of wine and glasses. They weren't fancy glassware; just simple drinking glasses good for carrying across the dark courtyard of the inn.

"My name is Garose," the innkeeper's son said. "I'm here to apologize."

He had the curiously clipped accent of the people who lived near the edge of the Marble nation.

"No need," said Annathea, accepting a glass. "I am Lady Annathea Long Reach, and these are my uncle and aunt, Sir Oliver and Lady Harrieta."

"I am pleased to meet you," Garose the innkeeper said. He parsed out the dark liquid from the wine bottle. "Even if the residents here had the right of things, the truth is that we live on trade. Chasing away business isn't good for anyone. It's not good for me, and certainly not for you. So on behalf of myself and everyone here, I apologize."

Annathea sipped her wine. It felt dark and cool in her mouth, and had a slightly spicy aftertaste when swallowed. "It's excellent wine," she said.

"Thank you. It's from our own vintner," Garose said. "I had hoped to convince you to buy a case or ten before you left."

"Consider me convinced," Annathea said, deciding to be charitable. "I'll take three cases."

"If you don't mind, may I ask where are you headed?"

"We're off to our home landing, the City-State of the Invulnerable Overlord," Annathea explained, feeling a pang of longing for her parents. Funny, she hated being around them, but now that she was away, she missed them constantly.

"This late in the season, that's not going to be possible with a group as large as yours. You won't make it to the Four Fathers' Bridge before the floods swamp the land," Garose stated.

"We know. Our course will be the Eastern road, into the Old Lands."

"That will certainly work, even if it takes a bit longer. Just keep your men ready for trouble," said Garose.

"Ghosts?" Sir Oliver said with a wry smile.

"Ghosts would be easy," said Garose. "You could hire a priest to bless you and your own. Or even to accompany you and put the spirits to sleep. No, the problem is that there's said to be goblins in the Old Lands."

"Goblins, you say?" Oliver said. He laughed. "No one's seen them since the days of the Dark Lord. They were crushed, broken, extinguished."

"Say what you will, but villages don't just hack and burn themselves to the ground. Someone or something does it to them."

Before Oliver could say anything else, Annathea spoke. "What do the golems say?" she asked.

"The golems are saying that the goblin raids are a minor thing. That their hunters will find and kill all the goblins soon enough. But it has been several years now, and the raids continue. Also, they never say anything about those who are doing it."

"That's weird," Annathea said.

"Maybe they don't want to cause a panic, especially with the war on," Harrieta said, looking up from her knitting.

"Maybe. Just be warned. I say you should keep your guard up and weapons close," Garose said.

"Well," Sir Oliver said, considering his own wine glass for a moment. "When I was young, I wished for the chance to test my mettle against the hated goblin foe. Now I might just have that chance, and it's the last thing I want to do."

"I'm not worried about it," Annathea said, raising her glass to Oliver and Harrieta. "I've got good people and more importantly, good mentors."

Garose raised his own glass in salute. "I've heard that you plan to leave in the morning. It's a selfish request in the hopes of more business, but please consider staying longer."

Annathea sighed. "Even if the brawl hadn't occurred, we had only planned to stay for a few days," she said. "The detour through the Old Lands is going to make our schedule very tight," she said.

"Well then, my lady, I wish you the best. I'll have the cases of wine delivered in the morning."

CHAPTER 25

VALLEY OF WIZARDRY

The Tower of Sorcery was at the center of the Valley of Wizardry. It rose up from the valley floor as high as the tallest mountain, nearly touching the puffy white clouds. Standing before a rainbow cast by rain on the other side of the valley, it shone in silver and white against the bluest sky. From where Wren stood at the end of the pass, many miles away, the Tower seemed perfectly sheer.

The only feature that he could make out was on the pinnacle. Upon the pinnacle stood a giant structure that Wren knew housed the Beacon. This wondrous device captured the light of the Creator as cast by the sun, harnessing it to bless crops, change the weather, and end disease and plague.

The Tower of Sorcery was the heart of the Domain of the Dryads, home of the Council of Arch-Magi, residence of the oldest and greatest of immortals. This

DANIEL ROY GREENFELD

was where Wren would be taught the secrets of magic, in order to become more than a man. It was his destiny.

Wren knew that the tower had stood since the Second Age, during which even the gods had stayed there. Raised by the greatest dryad artisans in the days before man walked the world, its role in legend and history was incomparable. Inside its smooth walls was knowledge arcane and mysterious.

Slowly, Wren began to notice the Valley of Wizardry itself. He could see that from the four corners of the Valley of Wizardry, roads crossed field, forest, and stream to meet at the tower's base. Even from a distance he could see that the flora were brilliant, lush, and well-tended, like a scene out of a dream. No field lay fallow. No section of wood seemed gray or drab. Every stream gleamed with speckled sunlight. It was heartbreakingly beautiful. Wren knew that the sight would be with him until the end of his days.

The four roads that divided the valley joined in a distant group of buildings comprised of white and bronze, at the base of the Tower of Sorcery. This was the Shining City, where travelers of all sorts from around the world came to pay their respects to the dryads. This far away, Wren couldn't really make out the details of the buildings. Minstrels had described the city as the greatest city in the world Perhaps it was not as large as some of the cities in the Golem Nations, but it was definitely more wondrous.

Facing the heart of the land, Wren knew that his life was about to change. His drab, dreary, miserable existence was going to be so much better going forward. He couldn't imagine cruelty being allowed in such a beautiful place, this heart of the world.

Here Wren looked forward to learning about ancient lore, allowing him to finally demonstrate to his family, fellow villagers, and even himself that he had value. He took a deep breath and walked with the others down into the valley. His legs and feet no longer ached. He had confidence in his stride.

They left the rocky path of the pass and walked down a great causeway. Made of giant engraved blocks of stone, its gentle grade made it possible for carts and wagons to enter and exit the valley with ease. It was like a bridge, except for its gigantic proportions and that it passed over land instead of water.

At the end of the causeway was a cluster of tanoak trees. The little army stopped to gather magic acorns for the evening meal. They were easy to carry and much more pleasant to eat than porridge. After every man had picked up their dinner, they continued in their march.

"Hey Wren!"

Wren turned and saw that it was Finch. The moment was ruined. Ram gave Finch a stern look. Finch swallowed, a look of worry crossing his handsome features.

DANIEL ROY GREENFELD

"What is it, Finch?" Wren asked.

"You're really going inside that tower?" Finch asked.

"Yes. I'm going to learn sorcery."

Finch smiled cautiously. "You know we just have fun with you, right?" he said.

"No, Finch. I don't know of any fun." Wren let some venom into his voice.

"Um...okay..." Finch said, uncertain. He swallowed. Then he spoke carefully and quietly, so that his voice couldn't be heard by any but Wren. "I care about Protea," he said.

Wren wanted to say something cutting and cruel to this chief of tormentors. He had waited his whole life for when he could give Finch his just dessert. Instead, all that came out was a loud "I hate you!"

"I'm trying, Wren. I'm really trying," Finch said. "I'm awed and inspired by the Tower. I wished that Protea could be here to see it and be as happy as I am seeing it. Thinking about making her happy makes me want to be kind to you. I was trying to make amends."

Wren wondered if Finch was being honest or playing a cruel game. Or, more likely, that he was trying to protect himself now that the Tower of Sorcery was in sight. He snarled at Finch. "Now that I'm about to become a great sorcerer, you finally want to make amends? You bring up my sister? You try to become friends?" he said.

"It's not like that!" Finch declared hotly.

"Yes it is. I hate you."

Finch sighed. "I'm trying, Wren. I'm really trying."

"You're just afraid that when I leave the tower I'll curse you," Wren snarled.

Another worried look crossed his old tormentor's face, which made Wren feel spitefully wonderful inside. Finch spoke quietly. "You're angry with me. I can understand that. Think on it, please. If not for me, then for Protea."

"You're just afraid," Wren teased bitterly. "You're going to reap what you've sown all these years."

Finch didn't say anything. He marched forward stiffly, not looking back. Wren was glad to have finally gotten him back after all the pain that he had caused. Deep inside though, Wren knew the feelings of fear that Finch must be feeling, and he had a wrenchingly uncomfortable feeling of sympathy for his old foe.

Wren looked over at Ram, who was looking back at him curiously. His older brother could sense his moods, but he often couldn't understand why he felt a particular way.

From the front of the long column, a horn blew a series of notes. Wren had heard that horn blowers could communicate detailed messages through their instruments. He wondered what was being said.

"Stop marching and listen up, lads!" shouted Sir Aethel from horseback. Wren could not help but notice that the knight-magistrate's kit, from his mail armor to his saddle and boots looked especially shiny today. Everything looked like it was carefully polished. His slightly receding blonde hair was carefully combed, and his face washed of dust. The knight, having left his squire back home, must have done all of these chores himself. Wren wondered why the knight was so particular about appearances.

Including Wren and the others from Perswald, about a hundred men stopped their march, as did the rest of the column. They still had about a quarter of a mile to go to reach the end of the causeway from the high Rockslide Pass into the Valley of Wizardry proper.

"It's not even early afternoon yet. I wonder why we stopped? And what's going to be said?" Wren wondered. Ram shrugged and took a drink from a water skin.

"Don't you know?" said Crow the storyteller from Grunswald. "The Valley of Wizardry is dangerous to mortals like ourselves. Only by staying on the road will we be safe."

"How is it dangerous?" someone else asked.

"Perhaps the dryads will tell us," Crow said.

Coming from the front of the column, the mated dryads Epiphron and Zelkova arrived on horseback. They split and stopped a good distance from each other. They also saw the other dryads spreading out along the length of the column. At perfectly equidistant places, the immortals stopped. Each addressed the men near them.

The dryad closest to Wren and his fellows was Zelkova. In the wondrous carrying voice of her kind, she said, "The Valley of Wizardry is dangerous to mortals. We will ride alongside the column to provide what protection we can. As long as you stay on the road and listen to our commands, you will live. Should you leave the road, you will likely perish before one of us can come to your aid. Should you survive, we will punish you for ignoring our warnings."

Her speech was echoed up and down the line by the other dryads. The men looked at each other doubtfully. Wren was brimming with curiosity about what lay ahead, but he knew that it wasn't his place to question the dryad overlords. It was often said that as much as dryads could be inhumanly kind, they could also be inhumanly cruel.

Stern warnings given, the long column of men began their march anew. The men took their last steps on the causeway and walked onto the cut-stone road. Wren looked down at his often-mended shoe when he took his first step in the valley proper. He felt a thrill as he realized that he had taken yet another step towards his destiny.

Wren grinned at Ram, who grinned back.

The air that they breathed tasted delicious, smelling of flowers and honey. Wren looked around. To either side of the road, fields of blooming plants of all sorts appeared in an instant. Honeybees and hummingbirds flew to and fro. A doe and her fawn looked back at him from the edge of the distant forest.

Surprised by the sudden change in scenery, the column ground to a jarring halt. Men cried out in alarm and quite a bit of fear.

"Where did these flowers come from?" Wren heard Finch ask. "While we were on the causeway, this was forest."

Wren blinked in shock. As he did so, he saw a flash of something very different from what he could see with his eyes. He decided to try his mage-sight again, looking through closed eyelids at the flowers around him. He closed his eyes.

Wren didn't see any flowers, nor could he see the doe and her fawn. Instead, there were trees. They weren't the same green-leafed, inviting woods that they had seen from the causeway. Instead of gracefully straight limbs, they had short, twisted branches covered with long thorns. Anyone who decided to leave the road to pick a bouquet of flowers would run blindly into the twisted limbs. Wren could well imagine how painful and confusing it would be.

He opened his eyes and smiled to himself. He was different. He had powers that the others lacked. If he wanted, he could leave the path and survive.

"As long as you stay on the road, you have nothing to fear!" Sir Aethel shouted. "Now…march!"

Reassured by the confidence of the knight-magistrate, they marched toward the center of the Valley of Wizardry and to the Tower of Sorcery. The countryside, be it forest, field, crop, or stream was hauntingly beautiful. The men commented and praised the land. They saw marvels such as apple vines, carrot trees, wheat stalks topped with berries, willows that actually wept, flowers with faces that watched them, and others things simply beyond their ability to describe.

They watched dryads tend their gardens, orchards, and fields. Their livestock was absolutely perfect, without flaw. Honeybees were striped with gold and silver. Billy goats had braids in their unusually long beards. Deer were herded like cattle. Geese and swans took the place of chicken and ducks. Sheep had beautiful coats. Horses and oxen pulled plows without the guidance of any master.

Sometimes the denizens of the land motioned the men to join them, yet none of the men dared to stray from the road. Enough of them had heard stories of those mortals who wandered into places where they were not meant to go. Those who were tempted were stopped by their peers or careful dryads.

They stopped at noon near a field covered with bronze-colored flowers that hung like bells from their stalks. When a breeze stirred the bells, they tinkled a chorus of wondrous music. Under the instruction of the dryads, the men walked into the field and picked three flowers each, cutting them at their base. These magical, musical plants served as their lunch. The flower petals were crisp, like lettuce but better. In contrast, the clappers were a strange combination of bean and nut. The stalks were edible, but they had a wood-like flavor that most did not find palatable.

They continued to walk through the course of the day. Periodically Wren would close his eyes and with his mage-sight see what was really there. Sometimes the land was just as attractive. In other places it was even more painfully beautiful. Then there were the scary things, like the trees covered with thorns.

There was one patch of field where the crops had stalks of gold. The leaves were white. As he watched, the green, berry-sized fruits of the plant began to glow. A terrible hunger coursed through him. He opened his eyes to see merely a well-tended field of green peas, yet his appetite remained. Hands trembling, Wren went frantically through his pack. He gobbled down what crumbs he had, and then what Ram offered. It wasn't enough. He wished he could stop for dinner.

He looked at the green peas. Even with normal sight they were quite tantalizing. He knew just a single bite would sate his hunger. Or would a bite end him? Hunger driving him, he fought a bitter internal battle against the desire to find out. He found himself to the side of the road, deliberating a dash to pluck one and come back.

"It's your decision," a voice said.

Wren jumped, startled. For a moment he stopped his march. In his hunger, he hadn't noticed that the dryad Zelkova had maneuvered her mount right next to him. He bowed deeply to her, as did the other men around him. Then he looked up at her, glancing at the tall, lean, unearthly figure of all of her kind. The green-brown thin vines serving as her hair had flower buds. Her face, beautiful but in an inhuman way that up close, did not stir him. Her berry-colored eyes looked down at him, unblinking.

To his relief, his hunger faded.

"My presence stops you this time, but next time? Perhaps I won't be there," she said.

Ashamed by her ability to recognize his weakness, he swallowed. "Yes, my lady," he said in a small voice.

"Little mortal, you have a gift," she said. "Perhaps even a great one. When using your gift, will you make the right decisions?"

"I believe so, my lady," Wren answered. "I'll be safe by following the commands and training of dryads."

"Nonsense," Zelkova retorted. "No leader can cover every contingency with commands. Also, the conditions that predicated the command can change. No instruction can guide you through all circumstances. When any of these cases emerges, you have to be able to make decisions on your own."

"Yes, my lady," Wren said.

"Your gift is part of you, even if in the future you do not want it to be. If you cannot make the right decisions for yourself, your kin, and your overlords, then your gift becomes dangerous," Zelkova said.

"Yes, my lady."

"Thus, if you want to eat what lies off the road, I leave that decision up to you."

"I don't understand, my lady." Wren was confused. What was she doing?

"You have to decide upon the right decision. You can stay on the road where you've been told it is safe and remain hungry until supper. Or…you can leave the road, pick some of those beans, and come back. I will not interfere with your decision. It is up to you to determine the right course of action."

Now the hunger returned. She had indeed been protecting him. He looked past her horse, and saw that the there were only a few more rows of this particular vegetable. If he didn't pick some now, it would be too late. He would have to either beg for food from his comrades or wait for the evening meal.

He knew there were dangers to his life and perhaps his soul, but one taste couldn't hurt, could it?

He started to take a step when a strong hand grabbed his arm, pulling him back. It was Ram. Wren struggled for a moment before giving up. His brother was right. He needed to stay on the road. He had been hungry for days when the season's yield had been poor. He could certainly survive a few hours. As they marched past the last of the dangerous bean patch, Wren's hunger faded.

"There will be times when your brother won't be there to protect you from yourself," Zelkova said, kicking her horse into a trot.

CHAPTER 26

SHINING CITY

"Look how tall and bright the Tower is compared to the city! I mean, any building in the Shining City is larger than our entire village, and the Tower makes them look like toy blocks!" Wren exclaimed.

The tower was at least a hundred feet wide. It was said to be two thousand feet tall. From a distance it was unbelievably impressive. Up close, it appeared like a gigantic smooth, white wall rising to infinity. Wren could see no lines in the tower, no marks and no opening except for the door at the bottom and the curious structure on the roof. Not even a water stain could be seen anywhere. Knowing that he stood in the presence of possibly the greatest handiwork ever made by a god was awe-inspiring. Only the work of the creator was more impressive, for that was the world itself.

DANIEL ROY GREENFELD

Ram grunted, muttering something unintelligible. On the walk through the strange and wondrous Shining City, Ram had hung his head lower and lower. He massive shoulders drooped; he dragged his feet when he walked. During the moments that Wren managed to tear his eyes away from the Tower of Sorcery, he had tried to comfort Ram. Wren had failed to cheer his brother, but he was too excited to worry about it. Deep inside he knew that he would feel guilty about it later.

"Aye lad, it's taller than any mountain," Sir Aethel said.

Sir Aethel, their overlord, had done the honor of escorting them through the hill that was the Shining City, and up to the base of the tower. That explained why he had made himself look very presentable today. "I passed through the valley here years ago when I was a boy. Never got to come into the Shining City though. Funny how even with everything being so bright we don't have to squint. It's not like white snow on a bright day."

The three mortal humans, Wren, Ram, and Sir Aethel had come in the company of dryads Zelkova and Epiphron. Without the presence of the dryads, they would never have been able to pass through the city gate, much less find their way through the incomprehensible maze that was the Shining City. Streets, bridges, and buildings crossed over each other in a way that seemed to defy geometry and geography. Everything was constructed of gleaming white marble, shining brass, and gleaming steel.

The denizens of the Shining City were mostly a mix of dryads, humans, and livestock, but there were other...things. He had seen creatures standing on two legs with striped fur all over their bodies, antlers, and cat faces. Horses were just one kind of mount: he had also seen riders on great lizards and birds. There was more, much more, and his head was swimming with the marvel of it all.

Even with his eyes open, Wren could sense the power thrumming through the air. The light here felt different. It was brighter, but not in a way that hurt his eyes. He didn't dare close his eyes and try to use mage sight. In fact, blinking hurt and he wondered how he would sleep tonight. He shrugged. These were problems that would be solved in the tower.

"I want to go with you," Ram said, sulking.

"You cannot. Only those invited may enter, and the invitation is not for you," explained Zelkova once again, with the eternal patience of the immortal.

Ram threw his big arms around Wren again for the hundredth time in the past day. Taking pity on his young vassal's misery, Sir Aethel clapped Ram on the shoulder. "Don't be sad," he said. "Wren gives you and your family a lot of honor."

Wren, Ram, Sir Aethel, Zelkova, and Epiphron, having made their slow way up the steep and maze-like streets of the Shining City, stood before a staircase that led up to a door at the base of the tower. Wren was tired, and a bit hungry, but ready for one last climb.

"From here on you must go alone. Walk to the top of the stairs and use the knocker to request entrance" Epiphron said. "May the gods bless you."

"Do not forget what I said to you about decision making today," Zelkova added. "You have the gift. Don't make me regret discovering it."

"Good fortune to you, lad," Sir Aethel said. "I'll see to it your brother does well. If he does half as well as the grandfather who earned the spearhead he carries, he'll be a hero."

Wren bowed to his superiors. Then he turned toward Ram, whose face had gone sour.

"Well, Ram, I guess this is goodbye for now," he said. They say the army marches in just over two months, so that's when we'll see each other again."

Again, Ram wrapped him in his arms. Wren didn't need the wetness on his cheek to know that his brother was terribly distraught. He felt a great sense of worry for his older, larger brother. Would Ram be okay?

"Look, it's only for two months," Wren soothed. "Then we'll be together again, as we always are. You'll be trained as a soldier, and I'll be a mighty magician. You'll have a sword, and I'll have a magic wand or something. When the war is done, we'll return home just as our father demanded, hero and wizard. It's going to be great!"

"Wren. I wish I could be there to protect you. You need me," Ram said. Wren was surprised. This was one of the longest statements he could remember his brother saying.

"Protection? That's nonsense, Ram. What protection do I need in the Tower of Sorcery?" Wren laughed. "Everything changes from here on."

Wren smiled at his brother. He bowed to Sir Aethel, Epiphron, and Zelkova once more. Then he turned to the stairs and took a first step. He felt a strange resistance for a second, but then he pushed through. The going became normal after a few steps. For a moment, Wren thought that the resistance was his imagination.

Then Wren heard a grunt behind him. Ram was trying to climb the first stair, but something unseen prevented him. His clothes and hair pressed on him as if he were walking through an incredible fierce wind. His brother shrugged off Sir Aethel's hand and kept making the attempt. Sir Aethel's face brow creased with anger at Ram's insolence. Wren knew he had to do something fast.

"Ram!" Wren shouted. "It's going to be okay. Promise you'll stay with Sir Aethel!"

"No!" sobbed Ram.

"You're going to get us in trouble! If I promise to come back in exactly two months, will you promise to follow Sir Aethel?"

Ram thought for a moment, then nodded and backed off his futile assault up the clearly enchanted stairs.

"I promise," he said.

Sir Aethel didn't seem inclined to punish Ram. Instead, he put his arm around the crying teenager. He nodded at Wren, who could think of nothing else to do but nod back.

Wren turned and climbed up the stairs. He counted as he went, reaching one hundred at the landing to the door to the Tower. The door, twice as tall as a man on horseback, was made of perfectly polished brass. Unlike the walls of the tower, it was rich with carvings and arcane writings. In the center was a bronze ring bound to the door. This was the knocker.

He felt scared. As an apprentice wizard, how well would he perform? Would the other students like him? How did the instructors punish failure? Would he be shamed, beaten, or cursed? He shook like a leaf. Could he just go back down the stairs and forget all of this? Maybe go back home. The dryads had never absolutely obligated him to come here to the Tower, had they? Would they let him turn back?

Wren looked back down the stairs. Ram was waving frantically at him. Sir Aethel saluted him with his sword. The dryads even nodded their respects to him. He was shocked. No one had ever paid him real respect before. It felt unusual, and good. He swelled with a pride that squashed his fear. Smiling, he waved at them.

Wren turned and grabbed the heavy brass knocker. He rapped it against the brass door three times. The door opened silently. It was dark inside, too dark to see.

"Come in," a voice said.

The voice was female, strong, and beautiful. The words seemed to make his legs move of their own accord, and into the Tower of Sorcery he went.

"Say goodbye forever to the old Wren," he said to himself as he walked over the threshold.

"As soon as I step through this door, he dies and the new Wren is born."

CHAPTER 27

HARNESS

At dusk, Abrog looked into the dead human smith's wicker cage. The man, once brawnier than any hobgoblin, was now a shrunken husk. During the day, he had curled up as if to keep warm in the sun and passed away.

This meant that the other two smiths would have to increase their pace. Abrog suspected that even with whippings the work wouldn't go much faster.

"Take them out and get them working!" he commanded.

A dozen goblins opened the other seven cages. Abrog watched his goblins use sticks to beat the humans out. The goblins were all now rather hefty for their breed, making the task seem trivial. Some of the humans cried and wailed, but off they went to their nightly tasks.

From dusk till dawn, they would be hammering, sawing, tending livestock, building, baking, cooking, gardening, sewing, knitting, weaving, and making all the things that Abrog wanted for his explosively growing tribe.

The problem was that they were going through slaves much too quickly. They got sick and died at a surprising rate. He would have to get more, and that would mean more raids. However, he suspected too many raids could mean that eventually the golems and humans would find his tribe's lair.

I need to find a way to keep my human slaves alive, Abrog thought. *Why is it that when goblins thrive, humans wilt?*

"That smith is not working! Use the whip," Abrog said, pointing at one of the two newer smiths.

The man was exceedingly muscular for his kind, with a build not unlike a hobgoblin. A goblin lashed the smith with his whip. After a single stroke, the man rushed to obey.

"When do you think they will feed us?" a newer, still-healthy woman quietly asked another in the human tongue as they sewed cowskins together. She had asked the question quietly, but Abrog had sharp ears.

"Tomorrow, if we are lucky," the other woman said. She was sallow-faced and extremely skinny, not unlike a goblin.

Abrog walked over to the captain of the goblin jailors. "Snard, feed the slaves," he ordered.

"Yes, Chieftain Abrog," Snard responded, sniveling appropriately. Abrog liked Snard. He had done well on several raids and had been promoted to the position of captain as a reward. Since then, the wiry goblin soldier had put on weight, so much that his belly was beginning to push out.

"Let's feed the filthy wretches!" Snard said to the goblin jailors overseeing the building of new wicker cages. His underlings cheered and rushed to obey. Through threats and use of sticks they marched their slaves to the tribe's cave. When the goblin masters and slaves returned, the humans carried baskets of food.

Led by their masters, the food-bearing slaves walked down the lane where the humans did their crafts and labor. They reached into their baskets and handed out food to the goblin masters watching each group of humans. Each goblin master would eat the majority of it, giving only scraps to the begging and pleading slaves.

A woman shrieked as a goblin tossed a scrap of unidentifiable meat down at her feet. She dropped to her knees and gobbled it up in seconds. Then she begged for more. The goblins laughed at her antics, and her master used his foot to push her backwards into the dirt.

Abrog turned his gaze to slaves who had been there for months. These were the wilted ones, whose bodies were so much skinnier, their heads hung low in a parody of rightful goblin posture. They never slacked in their work, but their pace was slower. When food was delivered, they never pleaded for more, simply picking up the scraps of food. They ate these precious scraps slowly, savoring every bite.

From the entrance of the cave bustled out the goblin cook, carrying a hefty human-wrought pottery bowl. He handed Abrog his morning meal and a broad headed spoon. In the bowl was mutton stew with bits of chicken egg and hefty chunks of meat. Abrog gobbled the stew down, feeling it sink comfortably into his belly. Since he had been eating well as chieftain, additional muscle had padded his frame to the point that he almost looked like a hobgoblin.

Hobgoblins. Muscles. Wilting humans, Abrog thought.

Why were the humans fading away? What was wrong? Abrog knew there was an answer. He just had to figure it out.

He closed his eyes and imagined that he was back in the days before he was chieftain. He remembered the squalor and trash of the land around the tribe's lair. He saw the wiry goblins and younglings of all ages performing the constant scraping for food. Without livestock or the human gardens, everyone had gone hungry and therefore stayed lean and skinny, except the burly hobgoblins.

Now Abrog opened his eyes and looked again at the slaves. The newer ones were solid, like hobgoblins or most of goblins of his tribe under his rule. The older slaves, on the other hand, were as skinny and slow as gobs and hobs.

Food, Abrog said to himself. *The slaves aren't getting enough. They are starving to death.*

The slaves worked for many hours every day for the leavings of goblins. By right of conquest the goblins ate more than their charges, but that right was literally destroying the means of how goblins were being fed. Just as the hobgoblin's consuming the majority of the food of the tribe had been terribly shortsighted, the goblin's denying the slaves an adequate portion was causing problems of its own.

In the early days of their human raids, it had been trivially easy to capture slaves. Now they were becoming more and more canny, using sentries and dogs, or travelling in large, armed groups. So far every raid had been a success, but Abrog knew from playing Bones and Stones that every player suffered a loss now and then. Even worse, his fear of a heavy golem/human attack on the lair could come to pass.

He stretched his imagination and thought about what might happen if the goblins ran out of their constant resupply of slaves. It would simply be a disaster. Without the humans, the livestock would die and the gardens would not grow. The goblins would have to scrape the ground again for grubs and tubers. The hunters would spend their nights finding game instead of watching the borders. He was very certain that there wouldn't be enough food for the entire tribe, and it would begin to starve. Abrog's minions would sneak meals made of gobs, hobs, and yearlings. They might even overthrow his rule.

All of this meant that Abrog needed to assign himself two tasks. First, Abrog needed to keep the human slaves alive. Second, he had to plan for if all the human slaves perished and he could gain no more.

Having finished his thoughts as well as his morning meal, Abrog handed his bowl and spoon back to the goblin cook. Then he bellowed, "Goblin jailors, to me!"

Once the ten goblin jailors assembled, he pronounced, "From now on, the slaves will not eat at the same time as goblins."

"Double meals for us?" said Snard, captain of the goblin jailors. "Thank you!"

"I did not say double meals," Abrog said, spearing Snard with his most fearsome glare. The goblin shrank under his gaze. "I said that you are to eat separately. The slaves will be given meals of the same size as the jailers."

The jailers recoiled. They murmured to each other. Abrog waited while they digested his latest command. Finally, they nudged Snard forward. He prostrated himself before his chieftain.

"Mighty Abrog, this is most unusual," Snard said. "Slaves and prisoners, if not meant for the pot, are supposed to find their own food. If they die, well, it was their fault for getting captured in the first place."

"Snard, that armor you wear, it was made by slaves," Abrog said. He snorted. "The whip you carry was also made by a slave. The chopper at your side? Forged by a slave who died today. The meal in your belly? Made with food grown by humans."

"Why does that mean the filthy slaves get more food?" Snard said. He looked up from the ground and sneered.

"Because, you dog-brained idiot, without the slaves we are made poor," Abrog said. He snarled, then roared. "Also, you mewling mouse, because I gave an order!"

Snard didn't even see the kick coming. Abrog could have killed him like he killed Skoldoh the night that he assumed leadership of the tribe. Instead he flicked out his booted toe, breaking the smaller goblin's nose.

Snard the goblin squawked, rolled back onto all fours, and clapped his clawed hands to his face.

"From now on, the slaves will be served separate meals. If any of their food is taken from them, I'll have the jailer who allowed it to happen beaten by hobgoblins. Do I make myself clear?"

"Yes, mighty Abrog." Snard said, holding his broken nose.

"What about the rest of you?" Abrog growled.

"Yes!"

"Absolutely!"

"We hear and obey!"

Abrog listened to the hastily shouted confirmations by the goblin jailers. He knew he would have to watch them carefully for a few days, but eventually it would stick.

The goblins and hobgoblins of his tribe had learned that those who followed Abrog's commands prospered, and that those who did not died at his hand. The bodies of those who did not obey became the main ingredient for stew the next day.

CHAPTER 28

YEARLINGS

Leading ten slaves laden with baskets of food, Abrog visited the yearling raising grounds. This was a clearing made not long ago, which was within a few hundred yards from the tribe's cave. This was where the young goblins and hobgoblins were kept busy practicing for war, learning hunting tricks. They also sang songs and played Bones and Stones. Otherwise the incredible curious youngsters got underfoot and into everything. In fact, Abrog had trouble faulting the hobgoblins for getting angry when the pests went through their belongings.

In the moonlight, the little ones saw Abrog, cheered, and ran to him with little decorum. In order to get the food Abrog's slaves brought, they needed to pay their respects. The yearlings prostrated themselves before him.

"Your loyalty does you credit," Abrog said.

The yearlings beamed at the praise, looked up to him with adoration. It was a far cry from the mix of envy he had felt towards the old chieftain, Izog.

"Slaves, dole out the food."

The slaves carefully handed out a small portion to each yearling, taking care not to get scratched or bitten by the youngsters.

The yearlings' goblin keepers couldn't manage to keep the looks of relief off their faces. They had to keep a close eye on their charges, because they knew Abrog recognized all of them. A missing yearling would mean harsh punishment for them. As the job of keeper was already a punishment in its own right, this meant that they especially dreaded whatever Abrog would cook up for them.

"They are large for their age," said one of the keepers. "Master, you were right about giving them food."

"Many of these are my progeny," Abrog said with pride.

Once his position as chieftain had solidified, Abrog had become receptive to hobgoblins in heat. He was certain that many a clutch of eggs laid had been quickened by his seed.

"Before I give you food, I have a question to ask the goblin yearlings," Abrog said to the assembled youth.

"There is no right or wrong answer to this question, just your own answer."

The youngsters peered up at him curiously from the ground. For a moment, he thought about including the hobgoblin yearlings too, but then he decided that he needed their adult size and ferocity for the battle line.

"Alright then, which goblins are bored here? Who wants to learn how to make things? If that's what you want to do, stand over by that tree," Abrog said. He pointed to a tall aspen tree with a thin trunk and high set of green leaves.

The young males looked at Abrog curiously. He knew that except for himself, most goblins were inherently lazy. Making things sounded terribly like work. Odds were that none of them would step forward.

To his surprise, several of the immature goblins jumped up and ran enthusiastically to the tree. They were followed by a slow trickle of more yearlings, taking a tiny portion's worth of the assembled males. Considering the large number of surviving youngsters in Abrog's new system, this was a good amount. Then, one of the little hobgoblins darted to join the small band of goblins.

Abrog walked over to the little hobgoblin, who along with the males shrank before him. He noticed that she found some courage, straightened up and did her best to stand proud before him.

"I'm as bored as any goblin here," she declared.

Abrog considered for a moment. This was the moment of truth for this youngling, when he would determine her fate. Was she meant to stand in the line of battle, or would she go down a unique path untried by any other hobgoblin.

"What's your name?" he asked.

"I am Skoldoh."

Skoldoh? That had been the name of a hobgoblin he had killed the night he had taken over as chieftain. It was a common enough name, but her behavior struck him as odd. The previous Skoldoh had raised her voice against him, and this one countered his command. He wondered if he should just kill her now, or try to marshal her independence in a different way.

Abrog liked challenges. He decided to keep her alive.

"You can stay here with the goblins," he pronounced, feeling pleased with himself.

She beamed with joy, baring her little fangs in the process. The male youngsters around her, enjoying the sudden relief of tension, jumped up and down around her.

Abrog stepped away to face all the yearlings. He raised his arms to the night sky and smiled a teeth-baring grin. As soon as the yearlings heard the tone in his voice they jumped, danced, hooted with glee. They knew what was going to come next.

Abrog commanded, "My next order will be followed absolutely! The penalty for not obeying me is death! My order is that you eat food!"

The slaves dropped their burdens of sacks of cooked meat chopped into hand-sized portions. They untied the cords that were keeping the sacks shut. The gobbers and hobbers, including the ones who had gathered at the tree, raced forward, each one seizing their portion before finding a place to squat down and eat their fill. None of them fought over a piece of food, as they knew that fighting would earn them a beating.

When they finished their meal, Abrog picked the selected yearlings out of the crowd. Other goblins would not be able to identify the unique youngsters in the crowd, but Abrog was no normal goblin.

He bid that they follow him. Together, along with the slaves, they walked out of the training grounds and to the base of the hill that contained their lair. They grew antsy, because in their gob and hob days they had been shut inside the boring, dull lair. They might have been safe from all predators, but they didn't see it that way.

They needn't worry. Instead of walking them past the slaves that knit, sewed, baked, hammered, sawed, smithed, and other tasks, Abrog stopped. For a moment he relished the sound of industry, of progress. Lead jailer Snard walked up to him. He sniffed through his bent nose, which Abrog had broken.

"Snard, have the slaves pay their homage to me," Abrog ordered.

Under Snard's shouted command, the dozens of slaves stopped their labors and prostrated themselves before Abrog.

Abrog turned to the small band of goblin yearlings and Skoldoh. "The slaves know things," he declared, confident the humans would not understand his words in goblin tongue. "Mysterious things like making good weapons and baking bread. Goblins should know these secrets. You will each be assigned a slave, and you will learn everything he knows. You will learn their language. You will help the slave in their tasks, and you will master them as a hunter masters their craft."

The yearlings were shocked for a moment. Incredibly curious, in the past Abrog had commanded them to leave the slaves alone; otherwise they would slow the slaves down in their tasks. Now they were being ordered to literally get under foot. In yearling fashion, they jumped, hooted, and danced. The jailers, on the other hand, traded odd looks with each other.

Now, in the language of the slaves, Abrog said in a loud voice to the workers, "I have brought you helpers. Assign them tasks and teach them your trade. If they do well, there will be extra food for you. Those slaves whose gob helpers fail to do well will be punished harshly."

Unlike most goblins, Abrog had no trouble reading the faces of slaves. He could make out the sense of concern that they felt. No matter, they would do as commanded or suffer the consequences. Such was Abrog's right to command, his right by conquest.

Days later, Abrog watched the increasingly healthy slaves trying to work with the adolescent goblins. The yearlings were earnest in their attention. The little workers found any task that suited their small stature very exciting. They weren't very good at anything, but Abrog hoped that this would change in time. Of course, there were still problems, such as misunderstandings and arguments. The jailers broke those up, liberally using the lash on both slave and pesky young goblin.

All in all, Abrog's plan appeared to be working.

The little hobgoblin, Skoldoh, was doing pretty well. He had assigned her to one of the smiths. Her stocky build would prove useful as she grew in both skill and stature.

Nevertheless, Abrog knew that they still had problems. These were the warm months when food was plentiful. When the snows came, he doubted whether his current number of farming slaves, gathering hunters, and raiding warriors could feed the rapidly growing tribe. He could try to cull the slaves, but then who would do the all-so-critical work that only humans could do?

The other option was to get even more slaves do more food making. Would enslaving even more address the problem, or would it make it worse? He knew that past chieftains had thought too many gobbers were a problem, but he was willing to gamble that they had been wrong.

As Abrog walked away from the growing industry of his tribe, he thought to himself, *I will need to raid for yet more human slaves.*

CHAPTER 29

IMPACT

Annathea trotted her horse back to her slow-moving caravan as it passed a patch of blackberry brambles. She beckoned to her uncle, Sir Oliver. He trotted his mount over. As he arrived she told him, "Up yonder is a clearing suitable for our needs. I'll lead the wagons in. Please see to it that everything is in place for this evening."

"I'm glad you found that clearing," Sir Oliver said. "Something about this stretch of woods seems wrong. All of the men and beasts feel it."

"I feel it as well," Annathea replied. "If the stories of goblins in Old Lands are true, then once the sun sets we must double the guard."

"Good idea, my niece," Sir Oliver said.

"That's milady to you," Annathea said, grinning.

Annathea led the long line of wagons that made up her caravan around the bend. There, just as she had said, was the clearing. She executed a wide turn, going completely around in a circle. As each wagon was placed in its spot, its horses were unhitched and allowed to graze. Men pushed the wagons close in to each other, making their wagon circle a primitive wall against attack. It wasn't perfect, but it was better than nothing.

The men hardly needed prodding to work on bettering their defense, dropping supply sacks in such a way that it would be hard to crawl under any wagon. They scrambled to the task with nervous anxiety. As Sir Oliver had mentioned, something was amiss about these woods.

As the sun sank to the horizon, the caravaners kept weapons close at hand. With the heat of day passed, the men started to put on what meager armor they had. While they weren't soldiers, they were trained with spear and crossbow to defend the wares that they moved across the land.

Annathea's aunt, Harrieta, kept the wives and children who travelled with the caravan at her wagon. If there was trouble, this meant that the men and unattached women would feel secure in the defense of their families. Harrieta was wickedly accurate with a crossbow, but she wasn't any good in melee.

Looking around, Annathea noticed several men were lounging before their chores were done. She walked up to them and said, "You two, picket my aunt's wagon."

The men stood up and fetched their spears. They didn't voice any complaint, and Annathea was glad. Her ability to lead was improving every year.

Large fires were lit to assuage the growing fear of the vanishing of the sun.

"My parents will be very unhappy to know we came this way," Annathea said to herself again. She had mused this very thought to herself a hundred times today. Perhaps she should have taken other roads, missing the City-State fair. No matter, what was done was done and they still had many days to go.

As the sun set, the smells of cooking fires wafted across their camp. Her stomach rumbling, Annathea circled the camp on foot, both outside and inside. Satisfied that there were no blocking trees blocking the field of sight from every wagon, she finally relaxed. Leaving her bow at her wagon, Annathea walked to the cooking fire by Harrieta's wagon. Sir Oliver was also there, and as the hot food was served, Annathea was first, followed by Sir Oliver and aunt Harrieta. Rank had its privileges, and first servings were one of them.

Annathea took her share to her wagon and sat on the driver's bench. Normally she would spend the meal chatting with her aunt and uncle, but tonight she just wanted a moment of quiet. The next week or so was going to be very challenging, and she needed to be composed. At least the clearing made it possible to watch the sun drop behind the nearby mountains.

Even as Annathea was absorbed into the beauty of the sunset, she noticed all the men turning their gaze to watch the sunset as well. Tonight it was a spectacular event, filling the sky with slowly changing oranges and reds. Just as the sun disappeared, the glow of the brilliant sky grew stronger and more radiant for a few wondrous minutes. Annathea forgot everything: the caravan, her betrothal, her responsibilities.

Impact.

Darkness.

Annathea felt the ground against her face, the blades of grass scratchy against her cheek. Her head hurt terribly. She was lying on her stomach, her hands painfully tied behind her back. She heard screams, shouts, and the sounds of weapons clashing.

She rolled to her side, began wrestling with the bonds, and witnessed disaster.

In the last remnants of the day, dark figures clambered through the tight spaces between wagons. The circle of defense had failed during the most beautiful moment of the sunset. The goblins hadn't waited until the dark that the legends claimed they craved. Instead, they attacked them in the caravan's single moment of complete weakness.

Now Annathea's people were dying, being slaughtered by screaming goblins of all sizes.

About half the goblins were large and squat, as large or larger than a man. These roared and shouted, charging at any opposition, wildly swinging clubs, mattocks, and chopping swords with nearly insane abandon. Their attack was so direct and blunt that the defenders hadn't a chance.

The other half of the goblins was hunched over, demonstrating a posture that would belong on an aged man or woman, not vibrant, howling monsters. Perhaps if they stood straight they might be as tall as grown men, but their posture meant that their heads were about four feet above the ground. With wily cunning, they would attack from all sides, stabbing and slashing from the flanks.

Annathea looked over at Harrieta's wagon. She watched as a cook tried to use her cooking fire as a barrier from a cleaver-wielding goblin. They circled around it in a mad, desperate comedy. The chase of the cook finally ended as another goblin joined the 'game'. Together, they pulled her down and Annathea watched as with practiced movements they tied up the cook. Straining they pulled their captive to where others were tied together, which was next to Harrieta's wagon.

Next to the wagon, Annathea saw to her dismay the prone, arrow-pierced figure of her aunt. Under normal conditions such injuries probably meant death. Here, death was guaranteed. Overwhelmed with grief, Annathea screamed her aunt's name.

Harrieta, who had been looking up at the stars, turned her head towards Annathea. She said something but was too far away to be heard. She coughed. Then she was terribly still.

"Nooooo!!" Annathea cried, ignoring the spike of pain in her head. She would miss her aunt, the lady who had changed her diapers, mended her hurts, and chaperoned her for years. She had been closer to Harrieta than to her own mother. The grief she felt was agony.

Yet the battle wasn't over. She could hear Sir Oliver calling the men to keep their circle together. Inhuman screams of pain and rage filled the night as the veteran warrior kept the goblins at bay. Annathea couldn't see the fight through the crowd of goblins, but she gained strength knowing that her uncle still lived. Sir Oliver not only lived but was holding his own.

"Who's ready to die next?" she heard his uncle taunt.

"I am coming!" a bass voice roared from the opposite side of the camp.

Then she saw him, the goblin leader. He crossed her camp at a calm walking pace, a tall, straight-backed figure carrying a dripping axe and shield. On his head, he wore a horned helmet. Annathea could only imagine the foul travesty that must be his face. The goblins parted quickly for him. Through the gap they made, Annathea could see her uncle for just a moment.

He and the men around him looked haggard, desperate, and worn. They were splattered with blood and goblin ichor. Yet she recognized in the face of Sir Oliver a resolute determination not to give up. The goblins crowded in, and she couldn't see her uncle anymore.

"Oh mighty Hyperion, king of the gods, please aid my uncle." Annathea prayed, her head afire with pain. "Let him kill the leader and break the goblins."

She couldn't see the fight, but she could hear the clash of weapons. She heard the cheers and shouts of the men and goblins watching their leaders duel. She worried, but not too much. Sir Oliver might not be in his prime anymore, but he was very well practiced. He was better than most men and certainly better than a mere goblin.

Annathea knew her uncle had failed when then the goblins roared and screamed in triumph. Knowing Sir Oliver was dead, she whispered to herself in despair, "By the gods, how could this have happened?"

"Give up your arms and you'll be prisoners," she heard the goblin leader shout.

"I'll be flayed in the abyss before that happens!" said one of her men, bravado filling his voice. Then there was the sound of metal chopping into flesh. The goblins surged forward.

Knowing all was lost, Annathea tried to free herself. Under her armor, in her bosom, she had a knife in her upper undergarments, but that was out of reach. She twisted and pulled on the knots to no avail. She had seen performers in the streets of the City-State free themselves quickly, but she didn't know their tricks. Ruefully she wished that the education her parents provided had included such things. If she made it out of this alive, she would pay someone good money to teach her the trick of escaping. Once she learned the skill, she would pass on that knowledge to everyone she knew.

The goblins quickly ransacked the caravan. The looters took what they could carry, focusing on weapons, tools, and dried foods first, and then luxuries. Considering what the legends said about goblins, this was incredibly disciplined behavior. Did this stem from the leader, the fiend who had killed Sir Oliver, or was it from some higher power?

She watched the leader walk around, pointing with her uncle's sword and clearly issuing commands. If the leader didn't obviously lead the goblins and speak their foul tongue, by his posture she would have thought he was a man. He had broad shoulders, a narrow waist, and the thick wrists of a swordsman. Yet the way he walked made it clear that he had never ridden a horse in his life.

DANIEL ROY GREENFELD

The horses! What about the horses? Would they be meat for the goblins? They ate everything, didn't they? She listened carefully and heard the horses. The goblins had attacked from downwind, a cunning move indeed. She had truly fallen into their trap. She felt awful for failing her people. She deserved whatever fate the goblins would meet out, but her people's single fault was that they trusted her.

Bands of goblins carrying collars, chains, and ropes were tying the surviving people of her caravan into a single line of captives. They worked in teams of five. Four goblins held a human's limbs while the fifth undid any armor and then did the securing. Again, the goblin leader demonstrated an unusual amount of discipline. More than that, he also showed incredible foresight.

The goblin enslavers came to her. She pretended to be meek until they were close. Then she kicked one in the leg. She aimed for the bony knee, but her riding boot connected with his shin. He screeched and danced in pain while his mates pinned her down, pinching and punching her. The one she had pained pulled a short, nasty falchion from its belt, and advanced on her. This would be the end. She closed her eyes and waited.

"Gluk Tlojk!" the bass voice of the leader said.

Annathea opened her eyes to find the falchion-holding goblin frozen with his weapon above its head. The leader came into view and looked down at her. His head tilted. Then he took off his horned helmet.

The face was a goblin's, but different. Even in the moonlight she could see that his dark-green mottled skin was smooth, lacking the pockmarks and warts the other goblins possessed. She wondered if he had ever suffered the acne that she had been plagued with in her adolescent years. His face was long, with almost painfully pointed cheekbones and jaw. The monster lacked any hair that she could see. His eyes were a sickly shade of yellow.

"You are female, yet wear the armor of a male. Why?" he leader asked.

His accent was perfect for the region, as if the people of the Old Lands had raised the fiend.

Annathea didn't answer his question.

"Either you talk, or I start killing and eating the children. Yours look especially tasty compared to the farm brats we usually get."

"You'll kill and eat them anyway regardless of what I do," Annathea said. She spat. "Rot in the abyss!"

The goblin leader grinned, baring a mouthful of fangs. She felt the goblins that were holding her down tense up, as if they expected something to happen. Then the leader closed his mouth and issued a series of

DANIEL ROY GREENFELD

commands. He walked away, and his underlings went to work on her.

Four goblins pinned her down, each using their full weight on a limb. With brutal efficiency, a fifth sawed away the straps of her armored vest with a serrated blade and then sliced off her dress with the cook's filet knife. She fought them, screaming and yelling, but each weighed as much as she did. Her struggle was futile. When the fifth goblin reached for her undergarments, she redoubled her efforts to throw them off. She refused the worst, hoping to be slain before the ultimate disgrace. His foul hands wrenched open her upper garments and stole the small knife hidden in her bosom. Then, to her surprise, the goblins stopped. They lifted her to her feet and marched, carrying her to the line of captives.

At least they had left her riding boots on, she thought.

A collar was clamped to her neck, which was tied by rope to the collar of one of her wagon drivers. In moments someone was tied to her collar from behind. Minutes later a sack filled with what felt and sounded like pots and pans was tied to her back, the ropes crossing like an 'X' across her chest, the cords biting into her now exposed shoulders. She was cold, nearly naked, and just another cargo carrying prisoner.

Even before the goblins had finished their looting the train of captives were marched out of the caravan and into the woods.

DANIEL ROY GREENFELD

CHAPTER 30

THE TOWER

Blazing light seared his head, waking him up screaming. In agony, he clutched his head and tried to squint his eyes to keep the light out. If anything, that made things worse. He rolled over onto all fours and fell off the bed onto all fours, knees smashing painfully into rock-hard floor.

Wren's eyes snapped open. He stared down at perfectly polished, perfectly smooth white stone. Eyes open, the blazing light faded away. Echoes of the pain in his head continued, but they were rapidly diminishing. He blinked and got a spike of pain for his troubles.

"Owww! That hurts!" he cried out.

For long moments he desperately tried not to blink again. He scrunched up his face in his effort to protect himself from the blinding light, gasping in pain when he failed.

"I hope my first lesson fixes my eyes," he said.

Standing up, he looked around. He stood in a brightly lit room not much smaller than his family's home. It had a shelf upon which a white-clothed mattress laid—his bed. There was also a chair, and a small table with a bowl of stew and a spoon. Built into one of the walls was a cupboard containing a mug. Beneath it was mounted a washing basin. Next to it was small hole in the floor for refuse.

All of it besides his mattress was made of the same perfectly polished, perfectly smooth white stone. Even the pipe of the refuse hole was made of the white stone, brightly illuminated all five feet down until its path turned out of sight.

How was the pipe illuminated if he was standing right above it? He looked around and couldn't find the source of light. Neither could he see a shadow, not under the shelf that was his bed, nor in the cupboard, nor even under the lip of the plate. It was as if everything was emitting sunlight.

The room was absolutely the strangest thing he had ever seen. Making it stranger was that he had no idea how he had gotten into the room. The last thing he remembered was walking across the threshold into the Tower of

Sorcery. That was all that he could remember, besides the fact that he had woken up just moments ago.

What was going on?

"Apprentice," a strong, beautiful, female voice said.

Wren whirled and looked at the source. Where there had been no break in the wall, there was now a doorless entrance to the room. Standing in it was an unusually tall lady dryad. She had hair that looked as if it were made of spun gold. Strewn through her hair were black flowers. Her face was lovely, yet as cold as stone. Robes made of shiny, white cloth hung from delicate shoulders, fringed with purple lace that shined like metal. At her waist was a belt that seemed to be woven from gold thread. From her hip dangled a long dagger with a jeweled hilt, which rested in a silver-leafed scabbard. In her right hand, she held an uncarved wooden staff.

He remembered his manners and bowed.

"I am Lady Eratea, arch-mage of the Tower of Sorcery, born of the Second Age. I am your master," the dryad said.

Her voice was as beautiful and as unyieldingly cold as the stone of the Tower.

"What is your name?" she asked.

"I'm Wren of Perswald."

"It is time to begin your transformation into a wizard. Come with me."

"Transformation?" Wren asked.

"Wren of Perswald, it is not your place to ask me questions. Do so again without my bidding, and you will suffer the consequences."

Wren shivered at her cold, inhuman tone. No shepherd would treat his flock in such a manner. In fear, he apologized. "I'm sorry, great lady," he said.

The dryad didn't respond. She merely turned around and walked down a white, stone hallway, which was as unmarked as his cell or as the outside of the tower. After a moment of hesitation, Wren followed. A few steps out of his cell he turned and looked back. The entrance to his cell had been replaced by another blank, featureless wall.

They didn't walk far. The corridor soon emptied into a square, featureless room. Inside, there was an attractive teenaged girl with carefully braided blonde hair. She was perhaps a year older than Wren. She wore a long white linen tunic and white leather sandals. Her pretty face showed no emotion to Wren, but her eyes flicked up and down him, as if measuring. In one hand, she held a carefully folded piece of cloth. In the other hand, she held a cup.

"You are to change into the tunic that Marigold is holding," Eratea said to Wren.

Wren blushed. Was this why the girl, Marigold, had measured him? He wanted to ask why, but he was wary of incurring the dryad's ire again. He sighed silently, walked over to the girl, and took the garment. He looked around for a private place to change, but there was none. There was also now no entrance into the room. It had been shut when he wasn't looking, leaving a featureless wall behind him and Eratea.

"Hurry up and change," Eratea ordered.

Wren stepped a few paces, positioning himself to place the dryad between him and the very human and attractive Marigold. He lifted his dirty, patched tunic over his head, the one from home. He slid the new one, marveling at the softness of the cloth.

He looked up and saw that the girl had repositioned herself to be able to watch him change clothes. He blushed and felt blood roaring in his ears.

The dryad made a motion with her ringed hand. One of the walls abruptly vanished without a sound. On the other side was now another room, one quite different from anything that he had seen so far.

In the center of the room was a circle of dirt in the floor from which small, curled vines grew. The floor, walls, and ceiling were covered with various arcane signs, scribed in what looked like black chalk.

"Take the cup from Marigold, walk into the room, drink the contents, and then quickly lie on the soil. Take care not to mar the symbols. Should you disturb them, you will not survive," Eratea said.

Wren nervously took the cup from Marigold. He walked into the room, stepping carefully through the symbols on the floor to the part that was just dirt. The symbols made his brain itch when he looked at them. He didn't understand why, but he wasn't going to ask any questions. He looked into the cup, guessing the liquid was wine. He hesitated and then gave a mental shrug. This was why he was here. The dryads wouldn't poison him. He swallowed the contents in one gulp.

It was the best wine that he had ever tasted.

If drinking wine was wizard training, then he was all for it. Suddenly light-headed, he flopped into the dirt with a chuckle. He felt sorry for the clean tunic now in the dirt, but clothes didn't have feelings, did they? Well, once he was a wizard, he would use a spell to make it clean in a trice. He decided at that moment to flirt with the girl. She was pretty, and he was the only boy here, right? He looked at her and winked.

Why was the girl looking at him with pity?

He realized that the dryad was chanting and pointing her staff at the ceiling. The vines in the dirt floor erupted into motion, growing, covering him, and holding him down. He wasn't too worried, although deep inside he wondered if he should be. He chuckled.

Eratea the dryad said, "The transformation isn't lethal, but it is painful. The drugged wine has temporarily paralyzed you, making it possible for you to begin the lesson without injuring yourself by struggling against the vines. Marigold will help you back to your chambers when it is over."

The dryad led the girl from the room. She motioned with her hand once they passed over the threshold. The entrance vanished, leaving Wren alone in the room. The arcane symbols in the room began to glow and dance. Wren thought they were lovely. He felt pinches all over his body and realized that the vines holding him were growing long, sharp piercing thorns. The pinches were thorns penetrating his skin, his flesh, actually touching his bones.

It began to hurt even through the numbness of the drugged wine. He suddenly felt wretchedly sober.

"Oww! This hurts! Let me go! Please!" he cried out.

In answer, the vines began to glow and pulse in tune with the symbols. The pulses seemed to penetrate past his flesh and bone and into his soul. He was in white-hot agony, scream after scream ripping from his throat.

All sensibility went away, blotted out by unending, unbearable, searing pain. The agony was unbearable and went on forever. It made it impossible for Wren to feel his body. The pain that racked his soul scorched the feeling of his physical being. It made it impossible to think, as his mind was overwhelmed.

Somehow a thought coalesced in the haze of torture that was his existence. What if this was the afterlife? What if he had died and gone to a place of eternal punishment? What if this was his fate for eternity?

Terror blazed in such volume that it matched his agony. It compounded the pain, the torture breaking through the walls of his sanity. Wren felt his mind and body crumble away.

CHAPTER 31

VISIONS

Wren danced with Cora around a burning barrel. They were joined now, the memory of their first chaste kiss playing across his lips. She crowed to the stars and he joined her. A flock of butterflies flapped their rose colored-wings past them, singing their joy.

"I was killed because of you," she sang to him with joy, her many rows of teeth smiling brilliantly. He was in love.

"My love, your name is strange for a girl. It's not the name of a flower."

She nodded. "I wasn't a girl," she said. "Now I'm a headless skeleton."

"If you like, I'll fetch back your head," he offered generously.

"If you do that, I would be very, very appreciative," she said suggestively.

Wren laughed to the world. Rabbits barked, trees howled, the wind danced.

She wept with joy.

Without warning, the searing pain returned.

Agony overcame him.

His ability to think or reason faded into the pain.

Wren stood under the branches of the giant oak, safe from the downpour. The rain was apples, smacking into the muddy ground. They rolled down the swells of the close-cropped meadow and into the low places. There, the apples pooled, rapidly growing in size.

Wren didn't like these apples. They were bitter, better for vinegar than for eating. The smell of their juice reminded him of home, of his mother using vinegar to clean and as a cure for various ailments. Home was far away. The homesickness he felt was overpowering.

Walking towards him was a man. The apples never struck the figure. Wren was jealous. He had always wanted the ability to avoid individual drops of rain. During drizzles he could somehow avoid any drops touching him, but a full-fledged rain would soak his

284   *DANIEL ROY GREENFELD*

clothes just as it would anyone else. Wren hated the man.

The man came closer, allowing Wren to see his dark, dirty patchwork armor. His helmet was dented. His boots were worn. His cloak was tattered. His sword was sheathed in a battered scabbard. By all accounts he appeared to be a vagabond, yet he was somehow more menacing than an angry Sir Aethel, or an emotionless Eratea. There was a finality with each step it took towards him. Wren squinted, trying to get a better view. The helmet kept the face in darkness. Only when the figure was near did Wren see the dark green skin. It wasn't the same shade as he had imagined, but he knew what came.

What approached was a goblin, except that its posture was straight like a man, not bent like a crooked old man. The minstrels had said goblins were bowed like old men, whereas hobgoblins had red skin and the posture of young men. Going by the stories of minstrels, this was something else.

The creature stopped under the branches, not ten steps from Wren. He couldn't make out the eyes. It rested one clawed hand on the hilt of its sword. The rain of apples kept pattering on the ground.

"I fight for my own destiny," the straight-backed goblin said, its voice deep and strangely accented. Not in a funny sounding way, but distinctly commanding.

"Who are you?" Wren asked, trembling with effort to keep fear out of his voice.

"I am the Goblin King."

Memories of childhood stories came to mind, all of them wrong. He had imagined Goblin Kings to be giant, misshapen creatures with horns, extra eyes, and long arms capable of taking off the head of a man with a single clawed swipe. Instead what stood before him was something lethal, perhaps besting the skills of Sir Aethel.

"Goblin Kings are no more. Turgon killed the last of them," Wren declared.

"Yet here I stand."

"Heroes always kill your kind."

"No. My people are fractious. Rebellious. More of my kind have been killed by kin than by the efforts of your heroes."

Wren nodded. He could well imagine the subjects of Goblin Kings rising up and killing their leaders. It made sense. So did the growing puddles of apples. They were linking up, creating giant pools stinking of vinegar.

"What can you do against the might of dryads and golems?" Wren taunted.

"What can you do against the coming flood?" the creature taunted back.

Wren looked around. The pools of apples had united, forming a sea. The wind stirred up waves, each larger than the ones on the ponds back home. In the distance, a giant swell appeared, closing slowly but with terrible finality.

Wren felt a bit of tantalizing fear. "What's coming?" he asked.

"Apples."

The swell grew into a wave. The wave was the height of a man, then the height of a house. Higher and higher it rose.

"Help me!" Wren screamed.

"You are beyond help." Unafraid, the goblin king turned to face the wave. "Perhaps I am not. We'll see."

The wave was now taller than the oak tree. From its crest, apples dropped into branches, creating an unearthly racket only matched by the roar of the surf. Then the wave collapsed onto the tree, splintering it and collapsing onto Wren. A thousand spikes of fire pierced him, pummeling his body, his mind, and his soul.

The last thing he saw was the goblin king, yet untouched by the tumult...

Agony overcame him.

A monster lived in his stomach. It was the monster that terrified children into staying under the covers. It made people carry lanterns in the dark. It frightened mortals and immortals alike. It was hungry.

Agony overcame him.

Wren was now crawling through a field of human bones, each of uncommonly large size. His arms and legs were clumsy, and he knew he could rise to his feet. Over on the next mound was something shiny. He crawled to it with the passion of a moth pulled towards a flame. Sometimes the bones snagged him, but each time he wormed his way free.

Now he was at the shiny thing. It was a small piece of gold. He tugged at it with his clumsy hand. It turned over, revealing that it was a mounting for a blood red ruby. It looked like it must have been part of a larger piece of jewelry.

Wren's arms, acting of their own accord, pushed the jewelry remnant into his mouth. Wren was horrified when he tasted the blood and decay on the piece. He tried to spit it out, but he was compelled to swallow. He felt it drift painfully down his throat.

At the edge of the field, bones shifted and started to move. More patches of bones began to behave this way, each one closer to him than the last. Wren wanted to get away, but his crawling was too slow, too inept. More and more of the bones rustled and stirred, closer and closer.

Somewhere in the distance, a woman yelled his name. The bones stopped moving. Wren crawled towards the voice. He found his limbs no longer clumsy and went to his feet. He walked towards the woman, who now called his name in his mother's voice.

Wren saw his mother, who seemed much younger than he remembered. He rushed toward her, as fast as he could run through the bones. She saw him. She screamed, clutched a swaddled baby to her chest, and ran. He chased after her and was on her in moments, turning her around with his bony claw.

"Don't take my baby!" she begged as the baby wailed in shared terror. "Take me instead."

He plucked the baby from his mother and peered down at it, right into the grinning face of a skull.

Agony...

Wren swam across a stormy sea.

Wren had never seen the sea or waves before, but he had seen ripples on a pond and heard stories about sailors and their ships. This matched the tales.

But the minstrels hadn't said that the rain scalded when it struck his skin. Nor did they mention the raindrops flaring up in flame momentarily as they struck the water. Once again, Wren wished for the ability to move in the space between raindrops.

Over the roaring of the storm and sea, Wren heard something new, something louder. He looked up. To his dismay, the ocean in front of him had caught on fire. He turned and swam in the other direction.

As fast as he flailed his tiring arms and legs in the water, he knew the flames would catch him soon. He was so scared of the flames that, in his fright, he couldn't quite make his limbs move effectively.

The burning surface of the ocean caught up with him. For a moment, he was in shrieking agony. Somehow he managed to take a deep breath and dive under the surface. The burning sensation lessened but did not go away.

Looking into the murky depths, he saw something rising towards him. Even before he saw it, he knew that it was terrible, dreadful. It was a sight out of nightmares.

Indeed, from the deep pit below rose a cloud of skulls. Like a flock of birds they moved in unison, driven by some sort of mad thought. They circled him, chattering insanely. Was this death, come to take him from the world above?

He should have been afraid, yet something about the grisly unfolding scene comforted him. Oddly he felt a bond with the skulls. Not kinship, but something else that he couldn't quite identify.

The chattering of the skulls increased in volume and they closed in on him. They bit into Wren's body, tearing the flesh from his bones. To him, it felt like caked dirt being scraped off skin, leaving behind something clean.

Naked of flesh, Wren felt free. He felt at peace, at one with himself. The trials of the body meant nothing anymore.

"Have I gone mad?" he wondered.

"No," he responded to himself. "I have merely begun to awaken."

Agony…

Pain…

Torment...

"I am Wren."

It was his first coherent thought in some time.

What a strange madness. He had seen vagrants in his village before. They had acted nothing like how he felt.

Did that mean his madness was personal? Or merely cultured by the forces that put him here.

Wren remembered that he had a body. That wasn't pleasant as he felt its pain, the same pain that echoed in his soul. He found that he could handle the pain in his body and soul by tiptoeing around it in his mind. He found cooler spots where he could find some measure of relief. He focused on this while his mind healed.

Eventually the pieces of his mind stopped coming together. There were parts missing, or changed. When he worried about it or couldn't handle the torture of his spirit, he conjured the memory of the cloud of skulls and felt at peace.

CHAPTER 32

TRANSFORMED

Compared to the clawing at his soul, the pain of thorns emerging from deep in his flesh was almost a delight. Then that pain faded too. The vines let go of him.

Wren found himself curled up inside a wooden cabinet. Hands reached inside and started to pull him out. Slowly, painfully, as if he had been lying in one place for too long, he unfolded as he came out.

His legs were weak and his vision blurry. He collapsed on the floor.

"Be strong and get up," a voice said. Someone stood above him. It was not Eratea, but it was a young female's voice.

Wren shook with the scars of pain and insanity. He felt like a shaky hatchling, still trying to find his strength and balance. He avoided looking at the girl while he was in such a state.

"The transformation is done," the girl said. Then she sighed. "Come on, let's get you back to your room. You might as well recover in more comfort."

With her help, Wren got to his feet unsteadily. "How is torture training for magic?" he asked.

She took him by the arm and led him slowly from the room, "That wasn't training. That was the transformation, where the dryads made it possible for you to use magic. They shaped you into a caster."

He looked down at his tunic, then hers. Hers was much nicer, with proper hems. It was cut to better suit her feminine figure. "Are you a wizard?" he asked.

"I am an apprentice. My name is Marigold. Unlike you, I am being taught spells and incantations. You are just a shaped caster, nothing more than a weapon of war."

"Does it get better than today?"

"You are mostly done. Next you'll be taught how to channel your power. That won't take long. Maybe a day."

"How long was I in there?"

"Several weeks. The cocoon kept you alive while you were turned into something else."

In shock, Wren looked at the cabinet, except that it wasn't a cabinet, but a giant, green seed pod on the floor. Inside the pod was enough room for him, if he curled up and didn't mind the thousands of thorns. He had minded the thorns. The pain that he suffered made him tremble. The dreams and visions that came along with it disturbed him. He knew deep down inside that the seed pod hadn't just given him the power to do magic. It had also changed how he felt and thought. His mind felt as if it had been shattered like a clay jar, then patched clumsily back together with horse bone glue. His body ached strangely too, and he knew that pain would never be the same again.

"Come on, boy. I have things to do," Marigold said.

Earlier in his life, Wren would have been shocked by her callousness. He was shaking, trembling, trying to hold onto his mind. Clearly she knew what he was going through but simply didn't care.

Marigold pulled him out of the room and down the hall, bringing him to his stark white room. She helped him sit on his bed. Then she took the chair for herself.

"I'm supposed to stay here for awhile to make sure you don't die."

"I don't understand."

She sighed, "One of my apprentice duties is to make sure that the transformed don't hurt themselves in the first few hours. You are valuable to the dryads, and the last thing they want right before the war is for you to kill yourself. For the next few hours, I'm your companion."

Wren was a teenager. He couldn't help but look up and down at her very feminine physique.

Marigold noticed his wandering gaze. "Just because I'm here doesn't mean I'm going to warm your bed!" she snapped.

"I'm sorry," he said. Somehow he doubted that she would forgive him, but he knew it was the right thing to do.

"I'll let it pass this time," Marigold said. "Consider yourself lucky. Some of the other apprentices would curse you with boils and rickets. I'm generous and kind."

Wren didn't think she was the least bit generous or kind. He kept this to himself and tried another tack. "I'm really sorry about…you know. Besides my sisters, I'm not used to talking to girls. And the last time I talked to one of my sisters was weeks ago. I'm really out of practice. If I say or do something stupid, please forgive me."

"If you say anything else stupid, I won't forgive you." She snarled, crossing her arms. "Just don't be rude."

They were silent for a while. He had questions about magic that perhaps she could answer.

"Can you cast spells?" he asked.

"Of course! I'm an apprentice with real training. Get off the bed and I'll show you."

Wren stood up. She took a deep breath, murmured strange words while making a pass with her hand. From the bed came a brief rustling noise. He turned to look at it and noted that the rumpled sheets were now perfectly smooth, almost crisp in appearance.

"No user of the arts should ever be unkempt," she said, as if reciting from a lesson.

"What else can you do?" Wren said excitedly.

"Magic isn't a showman's tool," she snapped irritably. "There are consequences for every spell that you cast. For mortals like ourselves, that is time. That little spell took a second off my life. More powerful spells take up more of our existence. I don't know about you, but I don't want to die young because you wanted to see tricks."

"Magic takes our life from us? What about the great wizards of legend? The ones who lived for centuries off their craft?"

"All magic has a price. The spells that the dryads use consume life force itself. When dryads cast these spells, they merely get tired. On the other hand, being mortal, we age and die. The way I see it, this means we have to be very careful with every meaningful spell we use. Who wants to die at the 'old age' of twenty?"

"That doesn't explain the wizards who lived for centuries…"

"Those wizard used magics that didn't come from the dryads. They probably sold their souls or something. As I said, all magic has a price."

Wren didn't know what to say. Learning how to be a wizard, to use magic, was turning out to be rather different than he imagined. Yes, he was being granted powers he never imagined, but at what price? He closed his eyes and sighed, filling his vision with chattering, calming skulls. Unlike before, the mage-sight didn't blind him. Instead he saw the normal darkness.

Wren's eyes snapped open. "Hey, my mage-sight is gone!" he said.

"You had the mage-sight before your transformation?" Marigold said, frowning.

"Not anymore," he said, feeling as if he had lost something special.

"Normally it takes months of training for it to develop," she grumbled. "If you had mage-sight before, it's still there. Just the transformation has changed it. Just try to use it, force it with your mind. Then it might come."

Per her instructions, Wren closed his eyes, tried to will the mage-sight back. Immediately it returned, blinding him as he gazed at the raw power of the inside of the Tower of Sorcery. He snapped his eyes open to relieve the pain.

"Whew. It's back," he said with relief.

"You have to close your eyes to make your mage-sight work?" She looked at him oddly, tilting her head, unfocusing her blue eyes to peer through him. After a few seconds, instinct made him blink. She nodded, "Looking at your aura, it's rather odd."

"What's an aura?"

"As you already know, if you use mage-sight then we can see magical essence. It gives off luminescence. People like us with the gift have an aura. People without do not."

"What is different about my aura?"

"It's not as bright compared to other casters I've met."

"Oh." Wren's heart sank. Once again he was weaker than others, this time in the one thing he hoped he would find strength.

"Close your eyes and activate your mage sight again," Marigold commanded.

Wren closed his eyes, steeled himself, and turned on his mage sight. The light around him was painfully bright. He felt the rushing presence of a headache. He focused on Marigold's glowing, sitting outline, which was a silhouette against the tower wall's brilliance. He could make out two glowing spots where her eyes would be. He looked downwards and realized that even though she was just an outline, her aura outlined a naked, very female body. Guiltily he snapped his eyes open and turned away.

"What's wrong?" she asked, clearly oblivious to what he had seen. Did that mean she didn't care about how her aura looked or did she see him in clothes? He didn't plan to find out, not from her. Not now.

"Um… it hurts to use my mage-sight here."

"Your eyes seem to suck in the rest of your aura," Marigold said. "I don't know what that means."

They were silent for a while. Curious about the future, Wren asked, "What now?"

"Tonight or tomorrow Lady Eratea will come to you and teach you how to harness your power. That takes a few hours. Then she'll let you go. You'll go fight in the war. Should you live, you'll get a stipend for your troubles."

"It will take me just a few hours to become a wizard? If that's the case, why are you still here serving as an apprentice?"

"Haven't you figured it out yet?" She said exasperatedly, "I'm learning how to become a real wizard. I can tidy up a house, heal injuries, and talk to plants. I'll learn a lot more before I'm done. You? You're just a transformed caster, a conduit for power. All you can do is destroy, and you aren't even good at that unless given a rod of power. No cantrips or spells for you."

Wren digested this information. It wasn't what he was expecting at all. He had thought he would learn magic and wisdom, when the reality was that he was a weapon, nothing more. On the other hand, with this power he would never need fear any bullying again.

Marigold sighed.

Wren could tell that she didn't like him and didn't want to be there. Still, he couldn't help but admire everything about her. She had such a lovely face, and her figure drew his eyes no matter what he did to avoid it. He had been attracted to girls who didn't like him before, but never had he a chance to sit and talk with them. If only he could say something that would make her like him!

Perhaps when he left the Tower of Sorcery everything would be different. He would return a hero after the war, and then the girls would line up to be with him. Their parents would gladly pay a dowry for their daughter to marry a wizard, wouldn't they? His wife would be beautiful like Marigold, with her long tresses and shapely figure.

Marigold coughed pointedly. Wren looked up with a start.

"Since you're so busy ogling me, it's clear you are fine," she said angrily, standing up. "I'm leaving. Don't kill yourself, or I'll raise your spirit from the dead and bind it to bird shit."

He nodded respectfully at the threatened punishment, but he knew it was a lie. What she described was dark magic, necromancy. Nevertheless it was a vile insult. To avoid invoking more of her ire he studiously looked away as she exited the room, the doorway vanishing as soon as she left.

Even though he was in the Tower of Sorcery, even with his so-called transformation, nothing had changed.

CHAPTER 33

LESSONS

Wren pointed the scepter. As instructed, he brought the pattern to the forefront of his mind. Energy was painfully pulled from his very soul, his very sanity. Deep inside, something screamed in agony, but somehow he didn't care that much. Once collected, he uttered the secret word and felt the power rush from the pattern, through the scepter and at the wall.

Lightning arced from the scepter and scorched the wall. Thunder echoed in the room.

"You have made the lightning cast three times," Lady Eratea said. "Yet I hesitate to teach you more. You drain yourself too much each time you summon the pattern within."

When they had begun what she had deemed his "first and only lesson", the dryad sorceress had said that it was acceptable for him to ask questions. Wren turned to Lady Eratea and asked respectfully, "Do you mean I lose part of my life, your grace?"

"Yes, a small portion of your life is taken each time you cast," Lady Eratea said. "It has been debated whether or not it is your mortal life span, or if it affects your destiny. However, the particulars do not matter, as the effect it is having on you is unusually dramatic. Instead of losing seconds or minutes per casting, you are losing years."

"What?!?"

Wren felt a growing numbness. He looked down at the wooden scepter, with the vine-bounded stone that was the dangerous end of the talisman. His emerging talent wasn't the salvation to all of his problems. It was killing him.

Considering his life to this point, nothing about this surprised him. Before the transformation he would have wept, been afraid, begged and pleaded with the gods. Now he had a strange ability to accept his fate. He realized he was giving up.

"Wren, I believe this is because your talent is incredibly marginal, or focused in other places. If you had other talents, in all likelihood, the transformation has blocked or destroyed them. Should you survive the war, come back to the tower and we will explore your talents."

"Perhaps I should avoid the war, just stay here and become your apprentice?" Wren suggested.

"Your talent is not strong enough for apprenticeship but can prove useful in the war. As for letting you stay here, I already have two mortal apprentices. For now I do not need another. No, you must go to war."

As always his hopes and dreams were dashed by his weakness. Physically he was weak and now he had learned he was magically stunted. How could one dazzle their friends if they couldn't cast spells without dying? He did not say anything aloud, but in his mind he knew his end would come on the battlefield. To his surprise, this did not frighten him.

"Come. My mortal apprentices, Marigold and Dayel, will see to your clothes, then send you on your way. You will be rejoining your overlord, the knight-magistrate." Lady Eratea gestured to the door, where the lovely Marigold stood with a tall, handsome young man.

Marigold was as lovely as ever, but her fellow apprentice Dayel was so good looking that he made her look plain. He was tall, athletic, handsome, and had slightly pointed ears. The male apprentice smiled casually at Wren, as if they were old friends. Wren knew from his smile that he was a good, decent person worthy of his trust."

"Thank you my lady," Wren said, giving his best low bow. Not only did he want to impress Marigold, but he also wanted to demonstrate to Dayel his competence and manners. At the dryad's dismissive gesture, he walked over to the apprentices. Dayel offered his hand, which Wren took. The handshake was just on the side of being painful, not that Wren really minded such small pain as a tight grip.

"Come with us," Dayel said, smiling with his perfect white teeth. Wren nodded and followed him and Marigold out of the chamber. He was led to a large staircase that circled down a giant, empty shaft. Once all three were on the staircase, Dayel snapped his fingers. The steps came alive, carrying them downwards. Wind rushed past them, and Wren wondered if this was how they had brought him into the tower's heights.

After a few minutes, the stairs slowed as they neared the bottom, finally depositing them safely at the bottom. Dayel stepped off, leading Marigold through a door. He paused to motion Wren to follow them through the door.

Wren followed them into a room filled with clothes along the wall. These were common tunics, trousers, and boots. Watching Dayel walk, Wren decided that he must have some small amount of dryad heritage, what the minstrels called "tree-blooded".

"I'll hold that," Marigold said, turning and taking the scepter from Wren.

As soon as she held the scepter, Dayel's smile faded, replaced by an expression of anger and malice. The taller boy stepped in close and buried his fist in Wren's gut. The blow dropped him to the ground, gasping for air.

"What a weakling!" mocked Dayel in a strong, commanding voice that any minstrel or general would cut off their right-hand to have. "Get up!"

Wren rolled onto his hands and knees. "Why are you doing this to me?"

"I could say it's because you looked at my girlfriend," Dayel explained with a kick to Wren's rubs. "But I'll be honest with you, I'm doing this because I can."

The kick rolled Wren onto his back. Marigold brought Wren's own scepter down on his legs, using it as a club to beat his shins and bare feet. Dayel simply kicked Wren in the arms and side, alternating his strikes.

Wren duly noted that the pain of receiving the blows from the other apprentices felt mild compared to the torture of the transformation. What did hurt was the knowledge that for all he had gone through to get here, he was still the target of torment, of humiliation.

What was the point of it all? Why had he gone through everything in his life only to get beaten and humiliated by others in what should have been his crowning moment? His life was a farce, a joke. Meaningless. To survive the war, he would die in the war an old man of fifteen. No one would ever care that he was gone.

Except for Ram. His brother would care. With his new power he could protect his brother. He could keep him alive even if it killed him. All he needed to do was get through this and return to Ram's side. That was his point in life.

The one thing Wren promised was that if he survived the war, he would find Dayel and Marigold and make them pay. He would make anyone who ever humiliated him pay for what they did to him. Unhesitatingly he would expend the last shreds of his mortal existence on giving them the justice they deserved. This he swore on his mortal soul.

Stoically Wren took the humiliation Dayel and Marigold heaped on him.

Their handiwork was careful, practiced. Clearly they had done this to others, because they did not mark his face or cause any real injury. When it became clear that they wanted him to beg and plead, he did so. He pleaded not because of the discomfort of what they did to him, but because he wanted to leave the tower.

After a while the beating was done. Panting, Dayel ordered, "Choose new clothes quickly."

Wren did as Dayel bid. He didn't examine the clothes too hard, because he knew that if he took too much time he would get another beating.

"Change here," Dayel said, pointing at a spot on the floor.

Wren choked down a deep sigh, again following Dayel's instructions. He blushed as he changed, hating every moment. Not yet done with their humiliation, the apprentices mocked his weak physique.

Then, through staircases and hallways, they took him out of the tower. Only when he stepped outside the tower did Marigold toss the scepter at his feet.

"Enjoy your pathetic, virgin life," Marigold taunted.

The great doors closed. Wren still did not show how he really felt. Inside he boiled with bitter anger at his constant humiliation, his constant torment, his lot in life. He hated that he was always a victim. The litany of his tormentors was endless, starting with Finch, Sparrow, Ox, the girls of Perswald, then the lady Eratea with her torture, the gods themselves teasing him about having a gift that would kill him. And finally Marigold and Dayel.

"By the damned stars, I'll make you pay," Wren swore. "Every last one of you. I don't know how, but as the world has caused me grief, I'll return it back to everyone. This I swear on my undying soul."

A thrill rushed out of his heart as the hate and bitterness rolled over him. For several long minutes, Wren stood there, relishing in unleashing his curse.

Then his shoulders sunk. What could he do? What power did he have to challenge the universe? His head hanging low, Wren walked away from the tower, into the Shining City. He needed to return to his liege and brother, Sir Aethel and Ram.

CHAPTER 34

CAPTIVITY

Annathea's head and neck spiked pain with each step. She suffered the worst headache of her life. The collar around her neck yanked her back and forth as the other prisoners on the chain stumbled. Her armor had been stripped off of her, and her undergarments were torn disgracefully. The ropes of the load she carried rubbed the skin on her shoulders raw.

Annathea shivered with cold and embarrassment. All that she wore against the night's chill was her undergarments and a smock that didn't quite go to her knees. Even that was torn, exposing the curve of her shoulder. She tried to hold up the fabric to cover her shoulder, but the shame of it all was dreadful. The smock itself was no comfort against the cold, for it was light enough to be worn under armor and dress. Yet she felt fortunate that they had left her socks and riding boots. She couldn't imagine making this walk barefoot.

Despair filled her heart. She had failed her caravan, her people, her aunt and uncle. At least half the people she commanded were dead, probably butchered for food. Goblins thought only of rape and conflict. She expected the worst when she arrived.

Somehow Annathea kept her head up high, if for no other reason than to boost the spirit of the other prisoners. They would take comfort if she fulfilled her role as noble leader. It was difficult, but in trying to keep her dignity and face in front of the others, she gained some measure of strength. This duty of hers was her lifeline, to which she clutched desperately. It would not be right for her to fall apart, so she forced herself to maintain the grace of a lady.

They walked long into the night. Exhausted, they were forced to keep going. If anyone sat down, the goblins beat them with whips until they stood up again. Annathea determined they must want fresh victims, that they didn't want them all dead yet. What better way to store food than to keep it alive? That's what humans did with livestock, wasn't it? Considering the savagery of the goblins, they must keep people as cattle.

If only they would just murder the ones who wouldn't get up, she would sit down and embrace the end. It would be a much cleaner death than what she could expect to experience in the hours ahead.

DANIEL ROY GREENFELD

Hours stretched into the night. The goblins set a fast pace, both the tall stocky ones and the more plentiful smaller hunched ones. She was already tired from a day's journey and slipped into a half-dream state of pain and fear. Her head, cloudy with fatigue and pain, barely noticed as they arrived at what seemed like a giant sprawling city of goblins. It was to the sound of hundreds of hooting, screeching goblins that woke her from her reverie.

They were paraded around the little city, the goblin chieftain showing off his prizes. The filthy goblins threw disgusting matter at the prisoners and her head was too foggy to even flinch. The stench of the place was mind-boggling. She tried to keep her head down, letting her hair cover her face. She gripped the corner of her smock in a tightly clenched fist, holding it up. Their march stopped and in a daze, Annathea nevertheless heard the heavy steps of the goblin leader.

The leader stopped right next to her. He grabbed her chin and raised it up, causing the pain in her head to spike. "Look over there!" he said, forcing her head to one side.

Annathea saw wicker cages holding children. Human children. In some cages, they were weeping. In others, the children were deathly quiet, with lost stares that looked somewhere else. As horrible as this was, she was shocked to see two human women assisted by several very small goblins, no taller than two feet tall, working together to build another cage. The women refused to look at Annathea or the other captives, but the small goblins leered at her.

Annathea hated those two traitor women more than she had ever hated anything in her life.

The other prisoners cried in horror at the plight of the children.

"I am Abrog! I am the chieftain of this tribe," shouted the goblin leader. "Serve me well, and you will live. Refuse to work, and a child dies. Hurt a goblin, and a child dies. Escape, and a hand of children die. Kill yourself, and two hands of children die."

It made it clear through gesture that a hand meant a count of five.

Abrog was keeping children alive to force people like her to help him and his tribe. It was diabolically effective. Annathea now understood why those women helped the goblins. With the children as hostages, how could they not? She couldn't even commit suicide without dooming ten children.

She felt utterly defeated.

Chieftain Abrog smiled at her with his lips sealed shut, hiding the sharp teeth in his mouth. They both knew he had won.

Annathea knew right then and there that all the stories about goblins were incomplete. The foul folk were described as stupid, murderous, raping, torturing fiends who deserved the kiss of steel. The reality of goblins was that they were much, much worse than imagined. They were cunning, violent monsters that used despair as a weapon. Against their will, she and her people would be forced to serve or see children suffer.

She refused to cry, shivering with the certainty this was only the beginning.

The chieftain motioned and the chain of prisoners were dragged around the wicker cages, past human craftsmen with goblin assistants at work in sheds. They were smithing, tanning, assembling armor, fletching arrows, preparing food, erecting sheds, and performing many other tasks. Curiously, the assisting goblins were more of the small ones. They moved with the energy of the young. Annathea realized with a start that the *young goblins were apprentices.*

Annathea knew something was terribly wrong here. Goblins were supposed to be near mindless and barbaric, almost a pest. They only became this focused when someone marshaled them. The Dark Lord had done so, as had other malignant forces in the past.

A cold logic crept into her soul. If something like that fiend directed the goblin chieftain Abrog, she needed to know who it was. Then she would escape and bring the weight of the Golem Nations down on it. Five children would die because of her actions, but across the land thousands would live. When the new darkness was destroyed, she would do repentance for the rest of her life. That is, if she lived until then.

They were herded into a wicker cage, each prisoner disconnected from the chain before being shoved in. She went in, and as the wicker door was shut and locked, pushed her way back through her people to the door.

"Who is your lord and master?" she demanded. She needed to know.

The chieftain moved close with speed, flowing across the ground with a cat's grace. Even with Sir Oliver's sword still scabbarded on his belt, the raw presence of the monster forced everyone back except Annathea. Abrog roared, "I am chieftain!"

"But who is your lord and master?" she mocked.

"Abrog accepts no lord and master," he said, his clawed hand darting through an opening in the wicker and grasping Annathea by the neck above the collar. He squeezed. "Do not ask again."

Choking, Annathea stared into his inhuman face. Curiously, it lacked the pockmarks that goblins shared. Darkness grew in the sides of her vision, and the world shrunk down to just his face. The moment before she was going to pass out, he let go, letting her collapse to the floor of the cage. She heard him stomp away. The other prisoners, once her hirelings and vassals, kept their distance.

Annathea slowly, painfully got to her feet. She straightened her smock. Modesty was everything. She lifted her head high. Then, in her most commanding voice, she declared, "Someone give me a tunic."

Her people hastened to obey.

CHAPTER 35

FIRST AMONGST SLAVES

From the mouth of the cave, Abrog watched the young goblins aid the human smith. They tended the charcoal fires, fetched wood, pumped the bellows, and performed every other needed task. The smith didn't like them, said they got in his way. Abrog ignored the complaints, as the smith was just another slave. The goblins stayed, worked, and learned. It might take a generation or two, but Abrog wanted to rekindle the old goblin passion for making things.

Legend said that in the days of the Dark Lord, the goblins had made many crafts. Not just weapons and armor, but machines that cleared forests, lifted timbers high, dug great holes, and burrowed into rock. Abrog wanted those days to happen again.

The smith's forge was outside the cave. In fact, in the few years since Abrog had taken the tribe, numbers had grown to the point that most of the goblins lived outside

DANIEL ROY GREENFELD

the cave. The raids against villages meant capturing food and livestock, which kept the tribe well fed. Of course, having banned the cooking of goblin kind, his tribe had grown rapidly. Encouraging more breeding helped the tribe's growth even more. Since goblins grew as quickly as any wild creature, in the span of just a few years his tribe had exploded in size.

A few reprisals from the golems had occurred, but the tribe's hunters had led them on wild chases far away from the camp. Even if they ever did find it, Abrog's captains would lead the survivors to distant rallying points. However, Abrog wasn't ready to test his minions against angry, stout golems. He was certainly not ready until he could guarantee overwhelming success.

The sound of chains rustling behind him caught Abrog's attention. A goblin jailer was pulling the special prisoner from the wicker cages. The prisoners were kept in them for their own safety, as it allowed more disciplined goblins to guard them from the hungry. This did wonders for keeping prisoners alive.

The prisoner had the long hair of a human female. She was now wearing a man's tunic over her shift. That shift had been torn and dirty but well-embroidered, marking her as the human leader.

"Your name, human thing?" Abrog asked in the language of the slaves.

"I am Lady Annathea of Long Reach. My father, Hugh of Long Reach, is a rich man. He would pay any ransom," she said, standing tall and proud.

"What can you do? My policy for adult humans is those with useful skills are kept alive, those without feed the cooking pot.

She considered for a second, then with head held even higher, said, "I am a lady. My skills are polite conversation, singing, dancing, and needlepoint."

"Then you are useless to me. Why shouldn't you end up as tonight's dinner?" Abrog had learned that, as with goblin kind, a simple threat was a way to get information or provide motivation. There was always the problem was that the information could be useless as the person being questioned wouldn't know the answer. Or would say whatever he or she thought Abrog wanted them to say. Fortunately, there was yet the person that could comfortably lie to Abrog. He could read anyone easily.

"You would be giving up my father's wealth," Annathea said.

"You know as well as I that your father would not trade with the likes of me," Abrog sneered. "For the last time, tell me why you should not end in the cooking pot."

The lady drew herself up and a look of proud resolution appeared on her face. At that moment Abrog knew she would offer him nothing. She was ready to die.

And yet...why was she ready to go into the pot? He had deemed her skills useless, but was that really the case? Normally people in her position of imminent demise became frantic with offers, none of them realistic. However, this female was behaving as if she would hurt him by dying.

Did she have a value he could not see?

If that were the case, then what was her value? Abrog thought furiously. If it wasn't her family anymore, it had to be something about her. She had no possessions on her, so that meant knowledge. Abrog loved knowledge. It represented power beyond the axe, spear, club, and arrow.

He thought back to her capture. He had seen the deference of the knight to her. The number of wagons on the road behind them had been full of blankets, beer, wine, bolts, tools, and crates of colored powders. The food stock was small, not the overstocking the goblins always did then squandered. The men defending the wagons had been better equipped than any group not escorted by golems his goblins had encountered thus far. Finally, unlike other caravans, there had been no merchant giving commands.

The deference of a knight and no merchant...

Things made sense. She was the merchant. The knight had been hers to command. Abrog laughed.

"You shall live," Abrog said to the lady. "You can do more than sing, dance, and needlepoint. You know how to command men and organize them. You know how to keep them fed so they don't waste their time scrounging. Teach me these things."

"Never! I will never help you!" Annathea said. She spat at him, her face turned dark with fury. The goblin holding her chains yanked them, doing it with such force that she fell in the dirt.

"You will teach me these things and everything else you know. Refuse to teach me and a human child will go into the pot every day until you do," Abrog said. He was bluffing, but there was no way that she could know his true intentions for them.

"I will kill myself before I help you!" she screamed.

"Then all the children will die and my goblins will feast."

The woman cursed him and struggled against the chains. While he laughed aloud in victory, deep inside Abrog felt for her pain. The human children represented so much potential in so much innocence. It was a cruel world, and he was just another cruel goblin.

DANIEL ROY GREENFELD

AUTHOR'S NOTE

Thank you for reading my book!

This is my first effort at writing a fantasy epic, but it's been a lifelong dream of mine.

If you have a moment, it would be a great help if you could write a review of this book on Amazon. You can make the review as long or short as you like, just so long as it's honest.

http://www.amazon.com/into-the-brambles/product-reviews/B00VC5UQHO/

If you want to send me your thoughts, or if you spot an embarrassing grammar or spelling error, please send me an email at pydanny@gmail.com. If you find an error, I'll credit you for your contribution when I update this book.

I blog about my fiction writing at danielroygreenfeld.com.

If you go past the afterword, you can read a preview of *Trapped in the Brambles*, the forthcoming next book in this series.

AFTERWORD

For as long as I can remember, I liked telling stories.

The earliest tale I remember spinning was at the age of six. I was at the dinner table of a friend, describing my family's adventures in Switzerland. They thought that I was recalling an exciting mountaineering vacation. Then I described how we were attacked by a pack of lions. My parents fought back, grabbing their tails and spinning them around their heads. To a six-year old, this is clearly how one deals with attacking lions.

Recognizing my penchant for telling stories, my parents helped me find ways to express this creativity. My father bought me a tape recorder. My mother would type my stories as I recited them to her.

As I became older, I found myself getting better at writing short stories. Novels were still intimidating to me for a long time, though. Half of it was just that getting down that many words was hard. But the other half was a lack of confidence. Still, the dream was always there.

Indeed, I wrote a book in my early twenties, simply throwing down my thoughts with pen and paper. Not being able to easily edit meant that the ideas were allowed to spring forth. Yet when it came time to copy the work into a word processor, I saw so many spelling and grammar mistakes that I thought my writing was garbage. I gave up.

In my late twenties, various people convinced me that I wasn't a good writer. I was told that my descriptions were bad, my characters flat, and my plots non-existent. Having been educated that I wasn't any good at writing fiction, I stopped. I gave up.

Twenty years went by.

In 2014 I returned to writing fiction. I decided to write a fiction book. I ignored the advice of those who said that I wasn't a good fiction writer. There are stories I want to tell, and the self-publishing revolution means that I can get my material out there on my own.

My change in opinion didn't happen in a vacuum. I had the encouragement of my loving wife, Audrey, my family, and the many friends that I've made in person and over the Internet. Without them, I wouldn't have started writing fiction again. I wouldn't have had the perseverance to write this book.

The people around you help determine what you can accomplish. There's a hard line between constructive criticisms and telling someone that they aren't good at something. Fortunately for me, the people I have in my life now are the kind of people who provide the former. Sometimes their constructive criticism can be hard to swallow, but never do they say that I'm not capable of telling a good story.

The moral of this exploration about my writing history is when it comes to creative endeavors, surround yourself with people who reinforce you, yet are honest enough to provide criticism that is constructive.

In closing, I would like to extend my thanks to a number of individuals who helped with the editing and proofing of this book. That includes my wife and main editor Audrey Roy Greenfeld, and my friends Philip James, Angel Alchin, Tomasz Paczkowski, Haris Ibrahim, and Chris Mahan. I would also like to thank everyone who encouraged me to see this through. I couldn't have done it without you.

PREVIEW OF TRAPPED IN THE BRAMBLES

Annathea looked at Abrog coldly. Being the master of a growing tribe, he was used to many kinds of looks. Her gaze did not bother him.

She had found a brown dress covered in the same layers of dirt that covered all the other slaves' clothes. This was good, Abrog thought. He didn't want her dying of exposure, not when she was so useful.

The dirt-covered brown dress that Annathea wore was plunder. It had been taken from a peasant girl's home, the previous owner probably dead. Faded, torn, cloth flowers were sewn in the cloth over her bosom, down the sleeves and along the bottom hem. Abrog could sense that the dress was an insult to Annathea, yet to the human males it was very appealing.

Like the other women, Annathea had hair that was loose, unbraided, and short. Her long braid had been harvested, cut off by goblin knife. Abrog knew that it had been made into bowstring.

Goblins hoisted another log into its hole, extending the wall another few feet. Quickly, several goblins tied the ropes that bound the log to its neighbor. Log by log, the entire camp would soon be surrounded by massive walls of logs, all on top of a continuous mound of dirt. It wasn't a castle, but it was better than allowing anyone to ransack his tribe.

Abrog was pleased with himself. This wall was something that the lady captive, Annathea, had taught him. In time he might have thought of it himself, but he was always so busy thinking and giving commands that it might have been many years before then.

Annathea was proving to be invaluable. As a noble lady, she hadn't just been taught the useless arts she claimed at first, but also logistics, construction, strategy, and basic siege craft. While she often didn't know the finer details of implementation, she was able to give Abrog enough information to piece together how to make things work with goblins.

Later, Abrog walked up to the men sitting in the wicker cages. As he approached, they stood up and backed away from his side. He didn't blame them.

"Who knows their letters?" Abrog demanded in the tongue of men.

The men didn't answer. That was to be expected for the new ones not yet broken to the yoke. Abrog nodded to the goblin jailers. "Fetch a young, strong slave," he said in their language.

The goblins cackled with glee. They opened a cage door and went in with their pummeling sticks. The men inside, weak from fatigue and hunger and scared of the dark, had trouble resisting the assault. The goblins grabbed a protesting young male and threw him face down to the ground before Abrog. Two of the goblins sat on his back and lower legs. The young male screamed in terror.

Abrog put his boot on the young male's neck, keeping his weight on his other leg. This was something Abrog hated to do, but it was necessary.

"If you know your letters, tell me or I start breaking necks," Abrog said in the human tongue. The young man squealed and begged.

There were fiercely whispered conversations amongst the men. Abrog slowly put his weight onto the young male's neck. His pleading turned into shrieks of pains and fear. Abrog clenched his fists, hiding what the young man's cries were doing to him.

"STOP! Back off! Get off of him!" roared one of the other male prisoners, shaking the imprisoning wicker with near insane emotion. This one was older, but not terribly so.

"Do you know your letters?" Abrog asked the young man.

"Yes, damn you, yes I know them."

Abrog took his foot off the young man's neck. He walked over to the prisoner claiming letters. "Speak to me the alphabet, in sequence. If you are wrong at any point, your friend here dies."

Abrog stopped just outside of where the lettered prisoner could grab him. Men (or goblins) in his situation sometimes displayed amazing strength and resourcefulness. Abrog was willing to stay his pride and keep back.

"Why do you need to know the aleph-bet?" asked the man.

"Because knowledge is power, human. Tell me now or I'll go over there and end his puny existence. Then his stinking remains will feed the tribe."

Shuddering, the man began reciting, "A...B...C..."

Abrog nodded, keeping pace with the man's recital. Then he asked the man to spell a number of words for him. They all matched what he had been taught by Annathea.

Satisfied, Abrog signaled the goblin jailers to return their charge to the wicker cage. Shaking and sobbing, the young male seemed happy to be out of their hands and back into imprisonment. The jailers would keep a close eye on him for a few days. Sometimes humans got over such humiliation, but other times they went crazy. Goblins and hobgoblins were so much more practical about these things.

The important thing was that Abrog had confirmed that what Annathea was teaching him was accurate. He thought as much, but so akin was literacy to what he knew of magic that he hadn't been certain he could tell if she was deceiving him or not. Fortunately for her case, she had been honest. He made his way back to where his most useful prisoner was chained.

Annathea looked up at his approach, hate in her eyes. He knew that in a heartbeat she would escape or kill him.

"Why do the golems not send many reprisal bands at once?" Abrog asked without greeting or ceremony.

"I don't know," Lady Annathea said woodenly, trying to hide yet another lie. It didn't matter, as Abrog could penetrate any of her deceptions.

"Do not lie to me. It does not become you," Abrog said, peering into her brown eyes. "Shall I have a child beaten?"

She glared for a moment, then folded. "The golems are at war," she said.

Abrog thought for a moment. If the golems were so busy with war, that meant that the host of goblins they were fighting must be gigantic. Perhaps their leader was a goblin king, bred true after so many centuries. Goblin kings had fought the dryads and golems for ages until the Dark Lord had appeared. The goblin kings weren't the type to serve as captains for even Him, so the Dark Lord had destroyed them.

"In which direction is the war?" Abrog asked.

"North," Annathea said.

"Impossible," Abrog sneered. "The dryads and golems would not allow enough goblins between their lands to embrace full-out war."

To his surprise, Lady Annathea laughed. She cackled at him. This infuriated him, and he bared his teeth in anger. He slapped her hard enough to leave a big red bruise on the side of her face. After a moment of being stunned, she laughed quietly and bitterly.

"Tell me what it is you find so amusing," Abrog demanded.

"You think your kind are so important. Yet all they ever have been are pawns in the hands of the mighty. Now your people are broken and weak," Annathea said.

"Tell me!" Abrog roared, hand raised to strike her.

She glared at him and didn't flinch. Abrog lowered his hand, respecting her courage.

"Dryads. The golems are at war with the dryads."

Abrog paused. Were not the golems and dryads friends? Why would they go to war?

"From what I understand, the war stems from a disagreement about who owns the Nesgath River. It's a major river that runs through both nations, ending in the Western Sea. Whoever controls it has an advantage in trade."

"Why? How does that work?"

"A large river like that is used to move goods across the interior lands and to the sea. Barges carry a lot more cargo than caravans. Whoever owns the river can toll anyone else to use it. There is great wealth involved."

"Why didn't this fight happen sooner?"

"There was a thousand-year treaty about use of the river that just ended, wherein the river was shared between the nations. The Granite Nation, my home, in whose lands we stand, had the lesser end of the deal. We tried to negotiate a new treaty that was more equal, but the Dryads refused to see reason. So it has come to blows."

"What is the view of the Domain of the Dryads? How do they feel about the equality of the suggested treaty?"

"They rejected it. They proposed their own that was worse than what existed before. Selfish leaf people," Annathea grumbled.

Abrog chuckled. Even Annathea took sides and had her prejudices against a race of immortals.

"Why have you not defiled me?" Annathea asked, abruptly.

"What do you mean? Have I not forced you divulge all your secrets?" Abrog asked in return.

"I thought goblins wicked, and yet none of you have tried to take advantage of me. Or any other woman, for that matter. We all remain pristine."

Abrog had no idea what she was talking about, "Pristine? You are not pristine. You are not clean. You live in the dirt and mud like everyone else."

She laughed bitterly in understanding. "My family would think me soiled, mated to you."

Now Abrog understood. He laughed, explaining when her face turned sour. "Hobgoblins mate with goblins to make more goblinkind. Why would we waste our time mating with humans?"

"Goblins mate with hobgoblins? How does that work? I thought all goblin kind were male," she said.

Abrog laughed. "That's an easy mistake to make," he said. "Goblinkind do not nurse as humans and other filthy animals do. After mating, hobgoblins dig a hole and bury their eggs there. Then, being stupid hobgoblins, they forget about where they laid the eggs. They hatch into gobs and hobs."

"Wait a second. Hobgoblins are female?" Annathea said. "That explains why you live together as a tribe, even though they're so different."

"I suppose so," Abrog said grudgingly.

"You do not seem happy about the state of things. Take you no ribald enjoyment in the process of mating?" she asked.

"We do not. For goblins it's unpleasant, yet because hobgoblins are so much bigger, we have no choice. When a hobgoblin comes into heat, the goblin closest to her is forcefully mated. It's very painful for the goblin. Often, we don't survive. I am different, for I am chieftain and command the hobgoblins to me, instead of me to them."

"So there is no desire on the part of goblins?" Annathea said. "No wonder why your people are so angry and violent. I mean, where is the joy of raising children and being in love?"

"Raising the young is for lesser beasts like animals, weak goblins, humans, golems, and even dryads. Being in love is meaningless," Abrog said proudly. Yet deep inside he wondered about her words. His people were weak unless a strong leader like him took command. Was it because they lacked the traits of affection and love that their communities were so small and self-destructive?

"Interesting," Annathea said. She sighed sadly, "The irony of all of this is that my family will assume that my capture means I've been violated. They'll never take me back. Yet here amongst monsters I am safer from the most terrible of humiliations than I am amongst my own kind."

Abrog considered. He did not like any of the selfish, greedy hobgoblins, but respected their strength and the necessity of their egg laying. On the other hand, he did enjoy learning from Annathea. She was smart, willful, and cunning. She wasn't dishonest by nature, but as a prisoner he had seen her carefully hide incidents by twisting the truth to protect her own.

For a few years now, Abrog had been manipulating human adults like Annathea by using their animal-like protectiveness of their young against them. He had always thought this a disadvantage for them, and in the short term, it was. However, in the long term it seemed that affection and love gave the enemies of his own kind a decisive advantage.

www.ingramcontent.com/pod-product-compliance
Lightning Source LLC
Chambersburg PA
CBHW071049250626
47159CB00002B/419

* 9 7 8 0 9 8 1 4 6 7 3 3 7 *